Elizabeth Gail and the Handsome Stranger

Hilda Stahl

Tyndale House Publishers, Inc., Wheaton, Illinois

Dedicated with love to the Teaters—
George, Carole, Phil, Renea, Becky, and Rachel

The Elizabeth Gail Series

Copyright © 1983 by Word Spinners, Inc.
All rights reserved

Cover and interior illustrations by Mort Rosenfeld

Library of Congress Catalog Card Number 89-50673
ISBN 0-8423-0806-7

Printed in the United States of America

96 95
9   8   7   6   5

Contents

ONE
The handsome stranger

Elizabeth stood on the high bank and looked down at the sandy beach and round, jewel-like Sparkle Lake. Her eyes were riveted on the boy standing alone, his profile to her. He was dressed only in blue swim trunks and he looked like a Greek god, or at least her idea of a Greek god.

She smiled gently and sighed as she folded her long, thin arms across her almost boy-thin body. The setting sun picked out golden glints in her brown curly hair. What would the boy do if she walked down to him and introduced herself? She flushed and frowned. How could she walk up to a handsome stranger and say, "Hello, my name is Elizabeth Gail Johnson and I think I'm in love with you?"

She stepped back and stumbled over a tree root. Awkwardly she caught herself and stood near the large poplar. She couldn't go find Jill yet, not until she'd imprinted the image of the handsome stranger in her mind.

What if he looked up and noticed that she was staring

at him? She stepped closer to the tree and the shade blocked out the hot rays of the afternoon sun. Just then he looked up and her throat closed tightly and her heart jumped. She could see that his eyes were as black as his hair. Finally he turned away and she sagged weakly against the tree.

She would not fall in love again! Last summer she'd met Kyle Grey and had fallen in love with him only to have that love fade away because of distance between them.

She laughed and her shoulder-length brown curls bobbed as she shook her head. How could she, of all people, fall in love with a handsome stranger? She knew better than to judge a person by his looks. Maybe her handsome stranger was mean and worthless. But then maybe his personality matched his looks. She could dream, couldn't she? Even though she was seventeen years old and on a working vacation with Jill Noteboom, she still had every right to dream.

As if her thought of Jill conjured her up, Jill walked toward the boy and stopped beside him and smiled at him, and the sound of her voice drifted up to where Elizabeth stood.

Sharp arrows of jealousy stabbed into Elizabeth and she wanted to run down to the beach and tell Jill to keep away from the handsome stranger, but she stood still and watched as Jill and the boy talked. He was just a little taller than Jill, who was tall for a girl. Maybe Jill knew the boy. Maybe she'd met him before when she'd been here with her grandmother.

Slowly Elizabeth walked away from the sparkling lake and the Greek god and her best friend. Surely the sun had affected her brain. She was a pianist; someday she would be a famous concert pianist. She wasn't a boy-crazy teenager who fell in love at a moment's notice! Or at the sight of a dark-haired boy with strong muscles.

Up ahead Elizabeth saw Jill's old red Chevy parked beside the Country Cafe. Three other cars stood in the parking area and Elizabeth wondered how Jill had been able to leave her grandmother alone to work in the cafe and gift shop.

Elizabeth stopped at the side of the road and waited for a camper to pass; then she hurried across the street to the small cafe. Maybe Jill had tried to find her to come work for a while. They'd both agreed to work to help Marabel Noteboom.

Just inside the Country Cafe, Elizabeth stopped and watched the short, slender, gray-haired woman bustle around from customer to counter. After her grandmother had called and asked for her help, Jill had expected her to be sick in bed, but she was healthy and alert and very spry. Elizabeth looked toward the gift shop where two women were browsing and she slowly walked over to wait on them. She and Jill had agreed to stay for three weeks on a working vacation. Marabel Noteboom had nodded mysteriously and said that that was all the time she needed.

Elizabeth rang up the sales and the women walked out, chattering happily. Jill still hadn't returned and Elizabeth frowned in annoyance. Marabel was Jill's grandmother. Jill should be here helping instead of walking around the lake with a handsome stranger.

"I don't think we'll have another customer," said Marabel as she walked toward Elizabeth. Marabel's blue eyes sparkled with excitement and Elizabeth could feel the tension in her. "Elizabeth, would you mind locking up for me so I can get a few things taken care of before it gets dark?"

"You run along. I know I can manage." Elizabeth smiled as she wished she could read Marabel's mind. Something was going on. In the week that she and Jill had been there, they hadn't been able to figure out what it was and Marabel wouldn't volunteer any information.

"See you later. Tell Jill not to worry about me." Marabel pulled her purse from behind the counter near the cash register, then lifted her small hand as she walked out the back door.

Maybe she had a boyfriend and didn't want Jill to know.

Elizabeth laughed under her breath. Jill would certainly be surprised if that was it. Jill seemed to think her grandmother should stay in her rocking chair at least ten hours a day.

At seven Elizabeth walked to the front door to lock it. Just as she reached for the knob, the door opened and Jill stepped inside. Jill's eyes sparkled and her cheeks were flushed red.

"Where have you been?" snapped Elizabeth as she turned the lock.

Jill's eyes widened in surprise. "Are you angry, Elizabeth?"

"Me? Angry? This is your grandmother's cafe and I came along as company for you, and you're off somewhere!"

Jill shrugged. "I'm sorry. I thought Grandmother was here with you." Jill looked around, then turned to

Elizabeth. "Where is Grandmother?"

Elizabeth forced away her anger. "She had some things to do, so she asked me to lock up."

"She had me lock up for her yesterday. What can be so important that it takes her away from here? I'd still like to know why it was so urgent that I come and stay with her a while to help her out."

"Maybe she just wanted to have you around."

Jill leaned against the counter. "Maybe." Jill suddenly stood straight, her face white. "You don't suppose she's just learned that she's dying and she wanted to spend her last days with me?"

Elizabeth shook her head. "Jill, your writer's imagination is getting away from you. You can't believe everything your head thinks up."

"You're right. You're right, Elizabeth. It has to be something else. But what?"

"Maybe we should spy on her."

Jill pointed at Elizabeth. "That's it! That's just what we'll do!"

"I was teasing! Jill, we can't spy on your grandmother. She's an adult and she can do as she pleases." Elizabeth gripped Jill's arm and shook it. "Listen to me, Jill! I can see by the look in your eyes that you aren't listening. I'd feel terrible if you forced me to spy on Marabel."

"So? Stay home. You can sit in Grandmother's living room and play Grandmother's piano while I find her and see what she's doing with herself when she sneaks away from us."

Elizabeth groaned and rubbed her hand over her head. Her curls flattened down, then sprang up again. "How are you going to find her, Jill?"

"This is a small town. I'll drive around until I find her." She walked toward the door and Elizabeth stopped her.

"Help me close up first and I'll go with you. I certainly don't want you getting into trouble."

"Maybe someone's blackmailing Grandmother and she has to go each evening to meet him and make a payoff."

"Or maybe she has a boyfriend and she has a secret meeting with him each evening at the same time."

Jill gasped. "No! Grandmother loved Granddad too much to marry again! Don't even suggest such a terrible thing." Jill rubbed her hands up and down her slender arms and shook her head.

"Hey, Jill, I was teasing," said Elizabeth, smiling. "Help me close up and I'll go with you just to keep you from getting too upset."

"How can I count money at a time like this? I want to make sure she's all right. Oh, I can't take this! I should have followed her before this, but I really expected her to confide in me. If she won't, I'll have to find out for myself what's going on."

Elizabeth opened the cash register and pulled out the bills. She didn't know what to say to Jill. Maybe she should ask about the Greek god just to get Jill's mind off Marabel. Elizabeth's hand trembled and she almost dropped the pile of twenties. She would not mention the handsome stranger to Jill!

Several minutes later Elizabeth sat in the passenger seat as Jill drove slowly through town.

"I don't know how you expect to find her, Jill."

Jill's eyes narrowed. "I'll find her if I have to look all night long! I know something terrible is going on and I want to help Grandmother all I can."

"What if she doesn't want your help?"

"She's going to get it anyway!" Jill slowed and turned right. Children played in their yards while adults sat watching. A few cars drove slowly on the streets. All the stores were closed except for a drugstore that looked almost deserted.

"It'll be dark before long, Jill. We might as well go home." Elizabeth rubbed her eyes, then strained again to catch sight of Marabel Noteboom.

"I want to drive around a little longer, Elizabeth. Please be patient." Jill drove toward the high school, then pulled into the large parking area near the football field. "I'll turn around and go back." She sighed unhappily. "We tried. If Grandmother won't tell me what's going on when I ask her tonight, then tomorrow evening I'll follow her and find out for myself." By the determined set of Jill's jaw Elizabeth knew Jill meant what she said.

Elizabeth sighed and looked toward the football field, then leaned forward, her eyes wide in surprise. "Jill! Look!" She caught Jill's arm and Jill stopped the car. "Isn't that your grandmother?"

"I can't believe it," Jill whispered as she slowly turned off the ignition. Silence surrounded them and finally Jill pushed open her door.

Elizabeth walked slowly with Jill toward the wide track that circled the football field. She shook her head in disbelief. Marabel Noteboom was dressed in a gray sweatsuit and was running around the track. Elizabeth had never seen a woman that age run so fast.

"She'll kill herself," whispered Jill in anguish as she

gripped Elizabeth's arm. "I've got to stop her."

"Wait!" Elizabeth caught Jill's hand and tugged her back beside her. "She looks as if she's having fun and she looks like she's been running for a while. She doesn't seem tired or winded, so this can't be her first time out. Let her run and then we'll talk to her."

"Running! I could see jogging, maybe—but running!" Jill wrung her hands and shook her head. "What will Dad say when I tell him his mother runs?"

"He'll be proud of her."

Jill turned, her face flushed with anger. "What do you know about it, Elizabeth Johnson? You don't have a grandmother—a *real* grandmother—to care about."

Elizabeth gasped and stumbled back a step.

Jill pressed her hand to her mouth and her brown eyes filled with tears. "I'm sorry. I didn't mean it."

Elizabeth swallowed hard to keep from crying.

"I never remember that you're adopted. It just slipped out. I know you have your Grandma and Grandpa Johnson. I know you love them just as much as I love Grandmother."

"Forget it, Jill," Elizabeth whispered hoarsely. "I shouldn't be so touchy about my past." Some days she forgot that once she'd been an unloved, ugly aid kid who was shoved from foster home to foster home. She'd lived with the Johnsons on their farm since she was eleven and she'd been legally adopted when she was thirteen. But she hadn't expected her very best friend to remind her of the difference in their backgrounds.

"I'm just so upset about Grandmother that I forgot myself, Elizabeth. Please forgive me. Please."

Elizabeth barely nodded and Jill finally turned to watch Marabel running around the track.

Elizabeth pushed her fingers into her back pockets and stood beside Jill and waited for Marabel to stop.

TWO
Surprising news

"Calm down before you talk to her, Jill," said Elizabeth softly as they walked toward the track.

Jill's face was as red as the tiny checks on her blouse. "I don't know what's gotten into Grandmother. She knows she's too old to run!"

"She'll hear you," hissed Elizabeth, jabbing Jill in the arm. It would be terrible to hurt Marabel's feelings. They stopped beside the track and Marabel jerked to a stop, her face red and her chest heaving as she gasped for breath.

"What are you two girls doing here?" Marabel rubbed the perspiration off her face with a tissue from a pocket of her jacket. "I didn't want you to know about this!" She frowned and shook her head. "You'd better not say a word to anyone! Do you both understand?"

Elizabeth bit her bottom lip and backed away from the short, angry, gray-clad woman.

Jill stepped right up to her grandmother. "What do you think you're doing? You can't do this again! I'll tell Dad!"

Marabel grabbed Jill's arm. She looked very short next to Jill. "You will not tell anyone! You spied on me and that's bad enough. If I didn't need you, I'd send you packing! But since you do know, you'll have to live with it. I run and I'm going to keep on running and you can't say or do anything to stop me!"

Jill gasped and Elizabeth couldn't believe this mild-mannered little grandmother could sound so firm and stern.

Marabel's blue eyes snapped as she looked from one girl to the other. "I want a promise from both of you to keep this a secret."

"I promise," said Elizabeth quickly, but Jill stubbornly shook her head.

"I don't want you to drop over dead, Grandmother! I want you to live <u>for a long time!</u>"

"Oh, Jill!" Marabel laughed softly and wrapped her arms around Jill's waist and hugged her. "I love you and I won't die. I'm not as old as you seem to think. Lots of people my age jog and run. I run because I want to. I just don't want certain folks to know yet. But they will when I'm good and ready for them to know." Marabel pulled Jill's face down and kissed her cheeks. "Don't worry about me, honey. I'm strong and healthy. I went to the doctor to make sure it was all right for me to run. And besides I have the Lord giving me strength and help. You see? I'm just fine!"

Jill looked helplessly at Elizabeth but she just shrugged. "All right, Grandmother. You have my promise. But I would like to know what's going on."

Elizabeth watched the two as they stood facing each other and she smiled to herself. She was curious to a point, but Jill's middle name was "Curiosity."

"I'll talk to you at home later," said Marabel, patting Jill's slender arm. "You two girls run along and I'll be home before dark. Elizabeth, you did lock up, didn't you?"

Elizabeth nodded.

"I don't want to leave you here alone, Grandmother," said Jill with a worried frown. "What if something happens to you?"

"Jill! I thought we'd settled that." Marabel tugged at her shirt collar, then patted her red cheeks. "I've been taking care of myself more than the eighteen years that you've been alive. I can continue to take care of myself. Run on home like a good girl and I'll see you later." Marabel turned to Elizabeth. "Take Jill home, will you? And keep her there!"

"You heard your grandmother," said Elizabeth as she caught hold of Jill's arm and tugged. "Be a good little girl and come with me." Elizabeth laughed softly and Jill glared at her, but followed her toward the car.

"You think this is a big joke, don't you?" asked Jill.

Elizabeth shrugged. "A little joke, maybe—but not big."

Jill jerked open the car door and slid under the steering wheel. "I happen to love Grandmother. I don't want her to be hurt."

"Running isn't your thing, Jill, but a lot of people run and they don't drop over dead. Let Marabel do what she wants and don't give her a hard time."

Jill spun the car around, the tires squealing. "Don't talk to me, Elizabeth. I'll feel the way I want to feel!"

Elizabeth looked out her side window with her head back and snapped her mouth closed tightly. She wouldn't argue with Jill. It wasn't worth it. Just then they drove through an intersection and the handsome stranger sat in a small white Ford at the stop sign. Elizabeth sat up and turned to look back.

"What's wrong?" asked Jill anxiously, slowing a bit. "Did you see something?"

Elizabeth flushed and turned back. "Nothing important."

Jill drove to Marabel's small house that stood just in back of the Country Cafe. "I could certainly use a tall, cold glass of Pepsi."

"I'll take 7-Up," said Elizabeth as she slid out of the car and stood to let the warm evening breeze blow against her. Strains of music and laughter and crickets blended together to make the sounds of a small town. It was almost as quiet as on the Johnson farm.

As Elizabeth walked beside Jill into the small house she felt a twinge of homesickness. Last summer she'd spent the month of July at Pine Valley Music Camp and now most of this month would be spent here with Marabel and Jill Noteboom.

Right now Susan, Ben, Toby, and Kevin would probably be watching TV. Vera would be cleaning up after supper. Maybe Susan had a date and would be getting ready to go out. Ben might be, too.

If she were home, would she be getting ready to go out?

She sighed and walked to the refrigerator for a 7-Up. She handed Jill a Pepsi and Jill walked to the small table and sat down. Elizabeth sat with her and sipped the 7-Up which she'd poured into a glass. Her mouth tingled and the bubbles tickled her nose.

If Jerry Grosbeck hadn't gone away for the summer, would he have asked her out?

She watched the clear liquid in her glass. He probably wouldn't have.

Oh, why was she thinking this way? She didn't really have time to go out much. Her time was spent practicing piano. It had to be that way since she was going to be a famous concert pianist.

Would the handsome stranger be impressed if he knew?

She flushed and quickly picked up her glass for another sip.

"Elizabeth?"

She jumped, then looked up. "Yes?"

Jill moistened her lips with the tip of her tongue. "I'm sorry for getting angry at you. I shouldn't have, but I was so upset about Grandmother. Forgive me?"

"Sure. I shouldn't have teased you when I knew how you were feeling. I know she'll be all right. Relax about it and maybe we can help her."

Jill grinned. "Sure, by running with her? Not me, thanks."

The phone rang and both girls jumped, then laughed as Jill reached for it. Elizabeth watched as Jill talked; then finally Jill hung up.

"It was a man," she said, her voice cracking, "for Grandmother."

"So?"

"He said his name was Pete Bogart." Jill locked her hands around her glass of Pepsi. "And he said he would be a few minutes late."

Elizabeth frowned. "What's wrong, Jill? Why are you upset?"

Jill's dark eyes widened. "Don't you understand? They have a date. A date!"

Elizabeth chuckled, then coughed it back at the look Jill shot her. "I think that's great, Jill. Think how lonely your grandmother has been the past few years."

Jill rubbed her forehead. "I know you're right and I'm being very selfish, but it's such a surprise. Running! Going with a man! What more will Grandmother do?"

The door behind Elizabeth opened and she turned to watch Marabel walk in. She groaned and rubbed her back.

"Give me a chair and something cold to drink," said Marabel as she limped across the room. "That last time around the track was too much."

Elizabeth held a chair and Marabel sank down, then leaned her elbows on the table and rested her face in her hands. She looked hot and tired. With a thankful sigh she took the glass of orange juice from Jill and sipped it with her eyes closed.

Jill frowned at Elizabeth as if to say, "I told you so." Elizabeth raised her brows and sat down next to Marabel. The tang of perspiration, a faint aroma of cologne, and the fruity scent of the orange juice filled Elizabeth's nostrils.

"You got a call a few minutes ago, Grandmother. It was Pete Bogart."

Marabel's head shot up and her eyes flew open. "Pete?"

"He said he'd be a little late." Jill's brows raised questioningly.

Marabel pushed back her chair and leaped to her feet. "Oh, my! I must shower. He can't see me like this!" She clutched Jill's arm. "I don't want you to breathe a word to Pete about my running. Understand?"

Jill nodded but Elizabeth knew she didn't understand.

"Give him a cup of coffee when he comes and keep him entertained." Marabel turned to Elizabeth. "Pete loves music. Talk to him about music, will you? I'll be out as soon as possible. And I won't limp a bit!" She limped to the hall and disappeared. Soon a door slammed.

"This is getting to be quite a mystery," said Jill as she slowly carried the dirty glasses to the sink. "It'll be very interesting to meet Pete Bogart, won't it?"

"If Kevin were here he'd be a detective for us and solve the whole mystery." Elizabeth laughed, then stopped abruptly at the look on Jill's face. "Sorry. I just wish you'd relax about this. You might like this Pete Bogart." She thought of the handsome stranger. "Maybe he's young and good looking. Maybe he's a salesman. You are only assuming that he's a boyfriend."

A few minutes later they walked into the living room and Elizabeth sat at the piano to play. She looked over her shoulder to see Jill at the front window, peeking through the white sheers.

"See anyone, Jill?"

She grinned sheepishly. "No."

"Let me know when you do." Elizabeth opened a book of best-loved original works by Tchaikovsky. Just as she touched the last notes, Jill gasped. Elizabeth spun around and waited.

"He's Grandmother's age! He doesn't look like a salesman or anything but a good friend. Look at him, Elizabeth." Jill's voice trembled and she motioned wildly for Elizabeth.

She peered through the window beside Jill and she watched the tall, strongly built man walk up the sidewalk. His black car stood on the street at the end of the walk. The man was dressed in a short-sleeved white knit pullover shirt tucked into gray slacks that fit snugly against the muscles in his thighs. His face and arms were tanned darkly and his hair looked almost silver. He looked toward the window and his eyes were dark—almost black. Elizabeth jumped back and hauled Jill with her.

"He might see us spying on him," she whispered sharply.

"He's absolutely gorgeous for a man his age," whispered Jill. "And he's coming to see Grandmother!"

The doorbell rang and they both jumped. Jill gripped Elizabeth's wrist. "I can't get it! You go. Please."

Elizabeth nodded slightly, then slowly stepped to the door and opened it wide.

"Hello," he said with a wide smile that showed off strong white teeth. "You must be Jill. I'm very pleased to meet you at long last."

She shook her head and swallowed hard. "I'm not Jill. I'm her friend Elizabeth Johnson."

"Oh! The pianist! I'm pleased to meet you." He took her hand in a firm grip, then released it and turned to Jill who stood with her eyes wide. "Hello, Jill. Marabel has told me so much about you that I feel I already know you. She said you're going to be as famous as your father."

Jill shook hands with him. "Please sit down, Mr. Bogart."

"Pete. Please, call me Pete." He smiled, then mo-

tioned for them to be seated first. They sank side by side on the couch and he sat back in a plaid over-stuffed chair. "Tell me, Jill, what are you writing now?"

She cleared her throat. "An adult novel. A mystery." She looked helplessly at Elizabeth.

"Marabel said that you like music," cut in Elizabeth. "Do you play the piano?"

He nodded. "But nothing like you. Who's your teacher?"

"Rachael Avery."

He whistled softly. "You *must* be good. I've heard her in concert often and she's excellent. I hated to see her stop to stay home with her family, but I could understand her need. Families are important."

"Do you have a family?" asked Jill stiffly and Elizabeth knew that Jill had wanted to ask if he had a wife.

Pete nodded. "I have two daughters and a son. They're married and live out of state. My grandson is here with me for the summer. I'd be very lonely without him around. My wife died about five years ago. But I do have good friends. Marabel is one of them. A very dear friend."

Elizabeth felt Jill stiffen but before either one could speak, Marabel walked in, dressed in a silky, flowered dress. She smelled like a flower garden. She smiled just the way Susan smiled at the boy she was currently in love with.

"Hello, Pete."

He pushed himself up and just looked at her. "Hello, Mari."

"Mari?" mouthed Jill and Elizabeth nudged her to keep quiet.

26

Suddenly Elizabeth thought of the handsome stranger and she wished she were standing with him, looking at him the way Marabel was looking at Pete, and receiving the same look in return.

She glanced toward the window and wanted him to be outside waiting for her to join him. Maybe tomorrow she'd see him again. Maybe then she'd have the courage to speak to him.

Her stomach fluttered and she leaned back and crossed her long legs and folded her hands in her lap.

THREE
Exciting rescue

Elizabeth lifted the paddle, laid it across the gunwales of the canoe, and looked around her. Had she really paddled so far away from shore? She dangled her long fingers in the clear, blue water and smiled, enjoying the soft feel of the water against her skin. Right now she was the only person in the whole world, at least on the lake. The drone of a plane along with the slap of the water were the only sounds. She looked up at the bright blue sky, watched the silver plane fly out of sight, and laughed softly. Jill and Marabel were wonderful, but it felt so good to be alone and away from their constant discussions and Jill's jealousy of Pete Bogart.

Elizabeth leaned back luxuriously, her face warmed by the sun and her mind drifting lazily. Soon it would be time to go in and help at the Country Cafe. Marabel was probably off running right now, knowing that Jill would open up. Elizabeth wrinkled her straight nose. She had told Jill that she'd work with her this morning.

Elizabeth leaned over the side of the canoe to look at her reflection in the clear blue water. As she did so, the paddle slid over the side and began to float away.

The paddle! Oh, no! How would she get back to shore? Elizabeth lunged for the paddle, trying to grab it before it got too far away. But she leaned too far and the canoe suddenly tipped, dumping Elizabeth into the lake. In a panic, she thrashed her way to the surface. Oh, how could this be happening to her?

She flipped over and a pain knotted her leg and she cried out. Water filled her mouth and she sputtered and coughed, then sank under again, the water closing over her head. She pushed up to the surface, her arms waving and splashing, gulped great gulps of air, then coughed and sputtered and choked. She looked toward shore and it seemed to be a million miles away. Her wet jeans and blouse were weighing her down. How could she make it back? Would anyone see her bright red blouse against the blue water and come and help her?

Tears streamed down her already drenched face and blended with the suddenly unfriendly water of Sparkle Lake. Oh, why had she come out alone? She thought of the life jacket, now pinned under the overturned canoe. Why hadn't she put it on? Now what would she do, all alone with a cramp in her leg?

But then, just as if the words were spoken aloud, she heard, "I will never leave you, nor forsake you."

The tears flowed harder. "Thank you, heavenly Father. Send me help right now. I don't want to die!"

Her head sank below the surface of the water and she frantically splashed to push up again. Her heart raced in alarm. Oh, she must not be afraid! Her lungs burned and felt as if they'd burst inside her.

Suddenly something wrapped around her neck and she fought and struggled. She wanted to scream, but she didn't dare open her mouth or she'd swallow the rest of the lake. She tried to kick, but the pain in her leg was too great. Water closed over her and she struggled harder. Was a sea monster trying to eat her for breakfast? What was she thinking? Was she losing her mind?

Just as her lungs felt as if they would burst, her head popped above water and she gulped in air. She clawed at the thing wrapped around her neck.

"Stop fighting me! I'm trying to save you!"

She gasped and turned her head and her eyes widened at the sight of the handsome stranger. His dark arm held her and she twisted and clung to him, sobbing and gripping and trying to get closer. He pushed her from him and she fought to get close again.

"You have to let me go! Trust me and I'll get you safely to land."

She stared at him and saw the kindness in his black eyes. She sobbed and forced her hands to let go of him. Her muscles were stiff with fear and she wanted to grab him again, but she managed not to. He caught her around the head and under the chin and pulled her after him as he stroked with one arm and kicked with both legs. She kicked with her good leg.

Would they make it to shore? Why had she struggled against him, tiring him?

They had to make it! She couldn't be a famous concert pianist if she drowned. Then she felt the sandy bottom under her heels.

"Try to stand," he said, gasping as he moved his arm to grip her around the waist.

She lowered her legs. Pain shot through her right leg and she cried out and grabbed him. "A cramp," she said in a strangled voice.

"Just relax. I'll get us out." He half-dragged, half-carried her to the edge of the water, then collapsed with her on the sand.

She shivered with cold and shock and he held her close. She pushed her face into his neck and great sobs tore from her, hurting her throat. She heard the gritty sound of the sand against her wet jeans.

"We made it," he whispered shakily. "Thank God we made it."

"Thank God," she whispered against the strong, brown column of his neck. He felt solid and strong and smelled like the lake. She couldn't move away from him. He was security and life. His arms were strong and firm around her. Finally she was able to lift her head and look into his black eyes. His black hair was plastered against his head and his lips were slightly blue with cold. "I . . . I think I'm all right now."

"Me, too." Slowly he helped her up and she carefully pushed her cramped leg straight until her foot touched the wet sand.

Finally the cramp eased away but still she clung to his neck and he circled her waist with strong hands. She lifted her face and smiled at him. Her hair was wet and sandy and hung in tails around her slender shoulders. "Thank you."

He smiled and her heart leaped. "I'm glad I was here."

"I thought I was all alone."

"I was up there." He motioned with his head to the

bank where she'd stood when she'd first seen him. "I saw you paddle out and I knew you were going too far out since you were alone. Then I saw the canoe flip over and I knew that you were in trouble." He shuddered and tightened his grip on her waist. "It seemed to take a year just to get to you." He pulled her close and pressed his cheek against her wet hair. "I don't want to live through that again."

"We're safe," she whispered. She rubbed her hands. "We're both safe, thanks to you. Thanks to God."

He moved so that only his hands touched hers and she twined her fingers with his. "My name's Seth."

"I'm Elizabeth."

"Don't ever go canoeing alone, Elizabeth."

"My leg cramped." She shivered. "I was afraid, but God sent you to save me."

"I'm glad." He had a wide mouth and a firm chin. His face and body were brown and she didn't know if it was his natural dark complexion or from hours in the hot sun. Muscles rippled in his shoulders and arms and chest.

She shivered, partly from cold and partly from being near him.

"You're cold. You'd better go take a hot shower and change your clothes."

"I know. I have to go to work at the Country Cafe soon."

He looked down at their hands, then slowly pulled free and she wanted to catch him and hold him and never let him go. She watched as he walked away. He was dressed in the same blue trunks he had worn the first time she had seen him. He turned as he reached the trees.

"Don't ever go canoeing alone again, Elizabeth," he repeated.

Her heart stopped at the look in his dark eyes. "I won't," she whispered around the tightness in her throat. "I promise."

"I'll meet you here in the morning and we can swim together," he said.

"I'd like that."

"About seven?"

She nodded.

"I have to go now."

"Me, too." But she didn't move and neither did he.

"I'm so glad you're safe!"

Tears filled her eyes and she blinked them away. "Me, too. And I'm glad you're safe, Seth. You are so brave!"

He shook his head.

"You are!"

He laughed. "Thank you. I'll see you in the morning."

"Yes. In the morning."

He turned to go, then turned back. "Seven in the morning is a long way off. How about tonight? We could go for a walk or something."

"I'd like that." Her heart leaped for joy. "I won't be free until about eight."

"I'll pick you up."

She didn't want to share him with Jill. "I'll meet you up by that tree." She pointed with a long, slender finger and he nodded and smiled.

"I want to know all about you, Elizabeth."

She flushed and suddenly felt very tall and thin and awkward. "I'd . . . I'd better go."

"Me, too." He smiled into her eyes and she felt

rooted to the spot. "I'll see you at eight."

"At eight." Her fingers twined around each other behind her back.

"Do you have a boyfriend?" She had loved Kyle Grey last summer, but he was too far away to keep the love alive. "No."

"Good."

She wanted to ask him if he had a girlfriend, but she couldn't force the words out. She couldn't survive if he said yes. With his looks, he probably had every girl around in love with him.

"I wish I didn't have to go, Elizabeth, but I do."

"Me, too." Jill was probably wondering about her, maybe even angry because she wasn't helping open the cafe.

Finally he turned and loped away and she watched until he was a speck in the distance. He had saved her life. He had held her and warmed her and calmed her fears.

The handsome stranger had a name now. He was flesh and blood and not a Greek god.

"I love you, Seth," she said softly. She flushed and looked quickly around. Farther down the beach several people were walking toward the lake, but they couldn't have heard her. But what if they had? Seth had saved her life and she loved him!

She lifted her pointed chin and squared her shoulders and walked up the embankment toward the tree where they were to meet at eight.

She stopped in the shade of the tree and looked toward the Country Cafe. Jill had talked to Seth. Did they know each other? What would Jill do if she learned about their date?

Elizabeth shook her head. She wouldn't tell Jill about almost drowning or about Seth saving her or about their plans. Her stomach fluttered. Jill was her best friend. Always before they'd shared every secret.

"Not this time," whispered Elizabeth with a slight shake of her head. She just couldn't take a chance. She loved Seth, and she needed him to herself. Jill would have to find her own boyfriend.

Elizabeth sighed then walked purposefully toward Marabel's home.

FOUR
New development

Elizabeth peeked around the antique clocks at Jill, who was waiting on customers at the cafe side of the store. Had Jill looked at her closely enough to know that she was in love, that she'd almost drowned but had been saved by the handsome stranger?

"Seth," whispered Elizabeth with her hand pressed to her flat midriff. Her nerve ends tingled. It was hard to keep Seth to herself and not tell everything to Jill as she had in the past. But she couldn't share Seth even with Jill.

"I was beginning to worry about you, Elizabeth," Jill had said when Elizabeth had finally walked into the Country Cafe.

"Sorry I'm late, Jill." Elizabeth had quickly walked to the gift shop part of the store and had picked up the yellow feather duster. Jill hadn't said anything more and Elizabeth had bit her tongue to keep everything back.

Just then the bell over the door tinkled and Elizabeth looked up to see a tall, lean boy with brown hair and brown eyes walk in. He was dressed in blue and white shorts with a matching tank top. He walked right toward her and something in his face alarmed her. She locked her hands together and waited behind the counter for him.

He stopped at the counter and just looked at her without smiling. "My name is John Bogart. Pete is my grandpa."

Elizabeth smiled hesitantly. "We met Pete last night." Was it only last night? So much had happened since then. "I like him."

"I'm sure you do." John looked down his thin nose at her and it made him appear to be a foot taller, but he was really only about two inches taller than Elizabeth. "He made me come in and introduce myself. We're planning a picnic and he said he wants you and Mrs. Noteboom to come."

"But you don't," she said in a low, tight voice.

"No, I don't. I think Mrs. Noteboom is after Grandpa's money and I don't like it at all."

Elizabeth's face flushed and she darted a look at Jill. If she heard what John had said, she'd be all over him and he'd never know what hit him.

"You are wrong, John," said Elizabeth coldly. "Marabel is a wonderful woman. She wouldn't marry anyone for money. I didn't even know she was going to marry Pete."

"Don't tell me that! You're her granddaughter. You must know."

Elizabeth leaned forward, her hazel eyes narrowed. "My name is Elizabeth Johnson. You've wasted all your anger on the wrong girl." She motioned toward Jill who was clearing off a small, round table. "That is Jill Noteboom."

He looked toward Jill and a flush crept up his neck and over his face and ears. He turned back helplessly. "I'm sorry. It's just that I can't stand to see Grandpa used."

"Marabel Noteboom is a wonderful Christian woman and she wouldn't use anyone! Why don't you get to know her before you make up your mind about her? If she does marry Pete, then you'll be getting a wonderful grandmother."

"I'm forced to meet her," John said gruffly. "Grandpa insists on us having a picnic together." John leaned against the counter and his breath fanned Elizabeth's cheek. "I might as well get it over with. Where is Mrs. Noteboom? I'll meet her right now and get it done."

Elizabeth opened her mouth to say she was out running, then snapped it closed.

"I'll be polite and nice if that's what's worrying you," said John sharply.

"Marabel isn't here right now. You'll have to settle for meeting Jill. But who knows? You might like her. She feels the same as you do."

He lifted his dark brows. "And how's that?"

"She doesn't want Marabel to marry Pete."

John stiffened and glared toward Jill. "You two will make quite a pair."

Elizabeth walked around the counter. "I'll introduce you."

Jill turned and waited, her fine brows raised questioningly. She was dressed in white slacks and a white and pink top. Her brown curls framed her slender face and hung almost to her slender shoulders.

"Jill, this is John Bogart, Pete's grandson. He came

to graciously invite us to a picnic."

"We won't come," snapped Jill, her brown eyes flashing as she looked into John's brown eyes.

"Why not?" he asked in surprise. "It's only a picnic. And we should get to know each other."

Elizabeth bit back a chuckle. These two were good for each other. She left them talking as she helped the only two customers. Finally they left and she walked back to John and Jill.

Jill said, "All right. We'll have a picnic, but I want to bring a date."

John shrugged and Elizabeth frowned. Who would Jill ask? Who did she know well enough to ask out? Elizabeth thought of Seth and she was ready to say she'd bring a date, too.

"That'll make it even all around," continued Jill. "Three couples. Elizabeth, you won't mind going with John, will you?"

What could she say? She was invited only because she was Jill's friend. "Not at all—if John can take it," she finally said.

"If you can take it, I can," he said. He smiled and she felt better and smiled also.

"Grandmother should be coming in soon and then we can settle on a time," said Jill in a very business-like voice. She looked toward the door as if Marabel would walk through at any second.

"I'll have a vanilla shake while we're waiting," said John as he sat down at a small table. His long legs barely fit under the table. "Would you girls join me?"

"I won't, but Elizabeth will," said Jill and Elizabeth frowned at Jill. "I'll fix the shake. Do you want anything, Elizabeth?"

"Strawberry shake." Elizabeth sat down across from John. She was dressed in pink slacks and a pink knit shirt with short sleeves and a small collar. Her hair was a lighter shade of brown than Jill's but the same curly style. Because they were both tall and slender with brown curls they were often taken for sisters, but their features didn't look at all alike.

"Are you out of high school, Elizabeth?" John folded his arms on the table and studied her.

"I have one more year. You?"

"I graduated this year. I'm going to Maine State in September." He was quiet for a while and he couldn't think of anything to say. "We want Grandpa to come live with us."

"Maybe he wants to stay here in his own home."

"He's lonely."

"So? He and Marabel should get married and they'd both have someone." Elizabeth folded and unfolded a white paper napkin. The buzz of the malt-maker almost blocked out John's gasp.

"You know how I feel about that!"

"You are wrong, John." Elizabeth leaned forward. "Pete isn't so old that he needs you to hold his hand. He's strong and healthy. He has a lot of years left and he should spend them the way he wants to. Not the way you or your family wants him to."

He shook his head. "You don't understand at all, Elizabeth. Two years ago Grandpa asked if he could come live with us, but we didn't have room and we had to say no. Mostly it was because of me. I was going through a rough time and I wasn't about to share anything with anybody. Now I want to make up for it. I want Grandpa to know we love him and want him. He's just being stubborn when he says he doesn't want to live with us."

"I don't think so, John. He and Marabel really do care for each other. You'll know as soon as you see them together. If they want to be together, then you should want that for them." Elizabeth gripped the napkin. "If you really love your grandpa, you'll want what he wants. Maybe you're forcing him to do something that will hurt him just as he was probably hurt two years ago. What if he went home with you just to keep you happy? Wouldn't that make you feel terrible? You'd regret it just as much as you regret not letting him come two years ago."

John swallowed hard as he rubbed a large hand over his brown hair. "I didn't expect this, Elizabeth. I thought I'd walk in here and ask the Noteblooms on a picnic, then grab Grandpa, and run to the nearest airport. But I see your point. I hate it, but I see it, and I do think I should see what Grandpa wants out of life, then tell him that's what I want for him."

Jill set the shakes on the table with a frown. "Did I hear you convince John that Pete and Grandmother belong together?"

Elizabeth sighed. "Sit down, Jill. I think I'll go find your grandmother so John can meet her. I sure can't win sitting here with you two."

Jill sank down on a chair just as Elizabeth pushed hers back and stood up. "Enjoy my shake, Jill."

Jill frowned. "Don't run off, Elizabeth. I might need your help."

Elizabeth lifted her hand and rushed to the door. The warm air blew against her flushed face and she breathed deeply to push back her irritation. How could Jill be so narrow-minded?

Several cars drove past but none of them pulled into the parking lot. A dog barked nearby and children ran along the sidewalk, calling to each other.

Elizabeth glanced at her watch. How could she wait until eight to see Seth? Where was he right now? Was he a permanent resident or on vacation?

Slowly Elizabeth walked around the Country Cafe toward Marabel's house. Maybe she could ask Marabel for time off to find Seth. She shook her head. What a daydream! The town was small, but there were a lot of tourists here, too. She'd never find Seth, especially since she didn't even know his last name.

She opened the back door and heard loud sobs coming from the kitchen. Quietly she walked into the kitchen, her throat tight. Marabel sat huddled at the table, her slender shoulders shaking with sobs. Elizabeth hesitated, then walked to her, and rested her hand on Marabel's back.

Marabel jerked and lifted her head and sniffed hard. "Oh, Elizabeth. I didn't hear you come in. Is something wrong at the cafe?"

Elizabeth sat down as she shook her head. "But I can see something's wrong with you. Can you tell me?"

Fresh tears ran down Marabel's cheeks and she shook her head and tried to rub away the tears. "My feet hurt and my back hurts and my legs feel awful!"

"Take a long bath and maybe you'll feel better."

Marabel sniffed hard. "I know. I'm just so tired and it would be very easy to quit running with Jill upset with me and all."

"Do you want to quit?"

"No! Yes. I don't know! My legs want to quit and my

feet would love it if I quit, but I set out to do it and I will do it!"

Elizabeth blinked back tears. "Sure you will. It's important to you, so keep it up."

"I wish Jill understood. It would help if I didn't have to fight her as well as my tired body."

"Pull yourself together for a little more trouble."

Marabel lifted her brows questioningly. "What is it?"

"Pete's grandson John walked into the store with a giant chip on his shoulder. He's with Jill right now and he wants to meet you."

Marabel sank back against the chair and closed her eyes. "Pete said he'd send John over, but I didn't think it would be this early."

"It's close to noon already."

Marabel's eyes flew open. "Oh, dear! I'd better hurry. But I'm so weary!"

"I'll go back and Jill and I will work until Sarah comes in at two. I'm sure Jill won't mind. I'll tell John that we can have a picnic tomorrow afternoon if that's all right with you."

"Fine. I'll call Pete later and work out the details." Marabel pushed herself up and groaned. "How can I do this to myself? Is it really worth it, Elizabeth?"

"If it's something that you want to do badly enough, it's worth it." Elizabeth thought of the hours and hours that she spent at her piano while others her age were having fun, and she knew it was worth it to her even though at times she wanted to join the others. "Don't give up, Marabel. Never, never give up on something you want to accomplish."

"Thanks, honey. I won't! These old bones can cry out, but I won't listen. I'm going to run!"

Elizabeth laughed and shook her head. "Good for you, Marabel! Good for you!"

Deep in thought, Elizabeth watched Marabel limp toward the hall that led to the bathroom. Why was it so important for Marabel to run?

FIVE
The picnic

Elizabeth walked from the piano to the front window and stood staring out. If she didn't tell Jill soon about Seth, she'd burst! How could she keep all her feelings bottled up? She wanted everyone to know that she'd walked and talked with Seth last night and swum with him this morning. She wanted to sit down with Jill and tell her every word, every detail so that Jill could share in her happiness. Maybe it would take Jill's mind off Marabel and Pete and the picnic that they were all going to in a few minutes.

"Oh, Seth," whispered Elizabeth, locking her fingers together in front of her while she stared dreamily across the sun-drenched front yard. If only she could've invited him to the picnic! But she was John's partner, thanks to Jill.

Elizabeth wrinkled her nose. John was all right, but Seth was perfect. He was very strong and could swim like a pro. And he liked her. She knew it and she shivered with delight just thinking about it.

She turned at a step behind her. "Hi, Marabel. Are you ready for the picnic?"

Marabel tugged her shirt over her brown slacks and wrinkled her small nose. "My legs hurt a little yet, but no one will ever know." Marabel tipped her head and studied Elizabeth thoughtfully. "Your eyes are sparkling and you look ready to pop. Are you that excited about going with John today?"

Elizabeth laughed and shook her head. She sat down and crossed her long legs and rubbed her hand down her jeans. "No, Marabel. I met a boy. He's wonderful!"

"Do I know him?"

"I don't know. I'll introduce you to him when we go out again. You will like him. I know you will and so will Jill."

"I will what?" asked Jill as she walked in buckling the belt of her jeans.

The doorbell rang and Elizabeth jumped up to answer it. She smiled and said hello to Pete and John. They were both dressed in jeans and short-sleeved pullover shirts. John glanced quickly at Jill, then turned to Elizabeth. Pete walked to Marabel.

"Everything we need is in the car," he said. "Shall we go?"

She nodded. "Jill's riding with her date. She said he'd be here soon."

"Don't wait for me," said Jill quickly. "We'll meet you at the park. We'll find you easily, I'm sure."

Marabel hesitated, then shrugged. "Lock up when you leave, Jill."

Elizabeth opened the door and walked with John to the car. Just who was Jill's date? It would be interesting to see. She wouldn't stay home just to show

Marabel what she thought of Pete and John, would she? Elizabeth frowned. She really didn't know Jill as well as she'd thought even though they'd been best friends for years.

"I'm driving," said John as he held the door open for Elizabeth.

She slipped in as Pete opened the back door for Marabel. John slid under the steering wheel, then turned and cocked his brow.

"Ready?" he asked and Pete said they were, then said something softly to Marabel that made her laugh.

Elizabeth peeked at John as he drove and she saw his jaw tighten. He didn't speak during the fifteen minutes that it took them to drive to the park and she didn't either. Occasionally she caught some of the conversation from the backseat.

At the park several people sat at tables or ran over the grass. Elizabeth watched children playing Frisbee and others badminton. As she helped John unload the picnic basket she saw a blue Frisbee lying in the trunk next to the jack.

"Want to play?" she asked John as she picked up the Frisbee.

He nodded. "Anything's better than listening to those two." He looked toward the table where Marabel and Pete stood side by side, holding hands and talking and laughing. "I've tried to accept the two of them together, but it's not possible."

"But you do like Marabel, don't you?"

He pushed the trunk closed. "Yes, I like her. And I'll admit I was wrong about her being after Grandpa's money, but I still want him to come live with us and make a home with us."

Elizabeth shrugged. "What can I say?"

"Nothing. I have to work it out myself."

"With God's help."

John picked up the picnic basket off the ground. "You're right, Elizabeth. I don't have to work it out alone. I do have God to help me. A couple of years ago I'd have laughed right in your face, but not now. I'm thankful that I'm a Christian and that I was raised in a Christian home. My folks stood by me while I went through a rebellious time. Now I want to make up for it."

"Is that possible, John?" She twisted the Frisbee around and around. "I know that when we sin, then confess our sin, that God forgives and forgets. I'm sure your family has done the same thing."

"Maybe." He shifted the picnic basket to the other hand and leaned against the back of the car. "You're good for me, Elizabeth. You make me think."

She smiled. "Thanks."

"Were you raised in a Christian home?" She gripped the Frisbee and looked down at the ground. A green gum wrapper lay near John's left foot. Finally she lifted her eyes to meet his. "My dad walked out on my mother and me when I was three. When I was five I was put in a foster home because my mother didn't treat me right. I was pushed from one home to another until I was eleven, almost twelve. Then I went to live on a farm with the Johnson family. They taught me about love and about God. When I was thirteen, they adopted me."

His eyes darkened with emotion and he gently touched her cheek. "And now you're a wonderful girl who's learned how to care about people."

Tears stung her eyes. "Thanks."

He smiled. "Thank you!" Just then he looked over her shoulder and the smile faded. "Jill's here. With her date."

Elizabeth's stomach tightened and she slowly turned. The Frisbee fell from her lifeless fingers as she watched Jill and Seth walk across the park toward the picnic table where Marabel and Pete now sat.

Seth and Jill!

Elizabeth stumbled back and bumped into John.

"What's wrong?" he asked in concern.

"I didn't know she knew Seth!" she whispered hoarsely. As she watched them Seth looked toward her, then stopped, his eyes wide in surprise. He had certainly not expected to see her here. Why hadn't he told her this morning that he had a picnic date this afternoon? But why should he? He hadn't declared his undying love for her. He hadn't said that he didn't have a girlfriend. But Jill?

"Is the guy special to you, Elizabeth?" asked John in a low, concerned voice.

She nodded, then wished she hadn't admitted it.

"Let's go say hello," said John, gripping her arm. "You can do it! You aren't going to fall flat just because some muscle man is going with your best friend."

Elizabeth lifted her pointed chin high. "You're right!" She walked with John toward the table where Seth and Jill were talking to Marabel and Pete.

"Hello, Seth," said Elizabeth with a smile that she hoped was natural. "It's good to see you again."

"Do you two know each other?" asked Jill in surprise.

"We've met," said Elizabeth.

"We're friends," said Seth with a smile just for Elizabeth. Was he trying to tell her that she was special to him even though he was here with Jill?

"Seth, I'd like you to meet John," said Elizabeth quickly, almost breathlessly. "John is Pete's grandson and he's here from Maine for a few weeks."

Seth held out his hand and they shook hands and John was polite as they talked.

"When did you meet Seth?" asked Jill for Elizabeth's ears alone.

"Just a few days ago. I didn't know you knew him." Jealousy shot through Elizabeth as she watched the expression on Jill's face as she looked at Seth.

Was Jill in love with Seth, too?

Elizabeth wanted to run away from the picnic table and hide somewhere until she could collect her scattered feelings.

"Isn't he wonderful?" whispered Jill and Elizabeth almost screamed in frustration.

How could she ever think that Jill Noteboom was her best friend? Did a best friend steal your boyfriend? Elizabeth flushed. Jill didn't know that she loved Seth.

Elizabeth looked quickly at Seth and he caught her eye and smiled back as if nothing was wrong with the situation. Was he remembering the precious time they'd had together in each other's arms after he'd dragged her from the lake?

"We were just going to play Frisbee," said John. "Want to join us?"

Jill hesitated, but Seth quickly agreed.

"I'll start the grill while you children play," said Pete as he poked around in the wicker basket.

Music from a radio drifted to them as they ran across the park to an area free of people. Elizabeth stood beside Jill and watched John and Seth run farther away. They stopped and faced the girls and Elizabeth couldn't take her eyes off Seth. Why wasn't he her date instead of John? What a special day it'd be if she were with Seth!

"I didn't know that you even knew Seth," said Jill sharply.

Elizabeth nodded. She had so much she could say, but the hard lump in her throat kept the words sealed in. She could see the jealousy that consumed Jill, and Elizabeth knew how she felt.

"I saw him first, Elizabeth," hissed Jill.

Before Elizabeth could speak, the Frisbee flew toward her and she jumped and caught it and sent it sailing back right into John's hands. He laughed and threw it again and Jill missed and had to run after it. Elizabeth watched Jill run and she wondered how she'd ever loved Jill enough to call her her best friend. Jill was certainly not a friend of hers! A band tightened around her heart and tears stung her eyes. She would not feel sad at losing a best friend! Jill wasn't worth even a tear! Elizabeth flushed painfully. What kind of a friend was she if she could suddenly turn against Jill because of Seth?

Several minutes later they all sat together eating hamburgers and drinking cold soda. Elizabeth crunched a potato chip and wondered if she'd be able to swallow it while Jill and Seth sat close together across the table from her. John bumped elbows with her and tried to get her into a conversation. Seth didn't act as if anything were unusual. Couldn't he feel the tension between herself and Jill?

Much later Elizabeth sat alone at the table and munched the last crumbs from the potato chip bag. Would the day ever end? Several times she'd tried to get alone with Seth, but each time Jill had kept them apart.

Elizabeth sighed and wiped her mouth with the back of her hand. Did Seth still intend to meet her in the morning to swim? Did Jill know about the plans?

Just then Seth stopped at the table and looked down at her. She bit the inside of her bottom lip and waited for him to speak.

"I thought you said you didn't have a boyfriend, Elizabeth."

She blinked in surprise. "I don't! John isn't my boyfriend. We barely know each other."

Seth smiled and sat down. "I'm glad to hear that. I'd hate to think we couldn't go swimming together anymore."

Elizabeth locked her fingers together on the rough top of the picnic table. Children shouted and laughed. Rock music blared from a car radio. "Seth, what about you and Jill?"

His black eyes widened. "What about us? I came with her today because she asked for my help. I couldn't say no, could I?"

"Did you know that Jill and I know each other, that we're both staying with Marabel Noteboom?"

Seth shook his head. "I almost fell over when I saw you here. But I couldn't just drop Jill. She's a nice girl and I wanted to help her."

Elizabeth studied him thoughtfully. Then smiled. "Do you spend all your time helping girls out of trouble?"

He grinned. "Just half my time, not all."

"Just how many girls are waiting in the background ready to grab you?"

"No more than a dozen, I'd say."

She laughed and he joined in. She reached out to him and he caught her hand and squeezed it.

"I must get back to Jill." He stood up and she felt like crying. "I'll see you in the morning at seven, Elizabeth."

She nodded, then watched him as he ran toward Jill. Elizabeth held her breath and gripped the edge of the bench. She would not be jealous of Jill!

SIX
Marabel's secret

Elizabeth's fingers flew up and down on the piano and the beautiful music increased her excitement. Seth had whispered that he'd see her at seven in the morning. Jill had looked suspiciously at them, but she hadn't heard what Seth had said.

"Elizabeth! Will you stop playing?"

She twisted around and stared in surprise at Jill. "Why?"

Jill rubbed her hands up and down her arms, her shoulders hunched, a haunted look in her dark eyes. "Grandmother isn't back yet! I think something has happened to her."

"She's running. She had a late start because of our picnic, so she'll get home late. Don't worry about her, Jill."

Jill flung her hands wide. "That's easy for you to say, isn't it? I *know* something has happened!"

Slowly Elizabeth stood up. She wanted to snap at Jill, but she forced back the sharp words. "Let's go find her and see if she's all right."

Jill nodded stiffly. "I'll go by myself."

"You're too upset to drive. I'll drive." Elizabeth could feel the strain between them. They'd had their fights in the past and then they'd made up, but this was different. Maybe they'd never be close again after this visit. After Seth. Her stomach knotted. Did she want that to happen? What could she do about it? Jill really was to blame for wanting to go with Seth.

"I hate running! I hate it that Grandmother won't . . . won't be content to relax and act her age!" Jill yanked open the door and walked out and Elizabeth grabbed her purse and followed.

The evening breeze was comfortably cool. A small dog somewhere down the street yapped angrily. Elizabeth started Jill's car, then drove toward the school and the track where Marabel ran.

"Can't you go faster?" asked Jill, her face pale and her hands locked together in her lap.

"Relax, Jill. Your grandmother will be all right."

"I wish we'd never come here, Elizabeth! I hate being afraid. I hate what is happening to us. And right now I hate Grandmother!" Jill's voice cracked and Elizabeth reached over and patted Jill's arm.

"We'll see about your grandmother and then we'll talk. We haven't talked, Jill, and we have to. But not until after we make sure that Marabel is all right." A band tightened around Elizabeth's heart at the thought of the serious talk that was ahead. How could she tell Jill that she loved Seth, and that she wanted him to herself? Jill would probably say the same thing. Then what would they do?

At the school parking lot Jill jumped out of the car before Elizabeth had the ignition shut off. With a frown Elizabeth dropped the keys into her purse and ran after Jill. The sky was a dark blue now and soon it would be evening. The large brick school building stood empty and silent. Jill's red car and Marabel's blue one were the only cars in the lot.

Elizabeth ran over the yellow marks painted on the pavement and tried to catch up to Jill. For someone who hated running, she certainly was speeding right along.

Suddenly Jill stopped with a muffled scream and Elizabeth was able to catch up to her. Elizabeth's heart leaped in panic at the sight of Marabel in a gray heap on the grass of the football field.

"I told you!" cried Jill, glaring at Elizabeth as if it were her fault that Marabel lay there.

Elizabeth frowned, then ran to Marabel's side, and dropped to the grass. "Marabel!"

Jill dropped on the other side. "Grandmother! Are you hurt?"

Marabel lifted her head and smiled a sick little smile. "Where don't I hurt?"

"Oh, Grandmother!" Jill's face flushed with anger and she shook Marabel's arm. "I told you!"

"Don't Jill," said Elizabeth sharply. "She needs help right now."

"I'm only resting. I hurt so much that I couldn't drive home yet." She clutched Elizabeth's arm and slowly stood up, groaning in pain. "I have never hurt so much in all my life!"

"Then quit this silly running!" cried Jill as she supported Marabel on one side while Elizabeth did on the other.

Tears rolled down Marabel's red cheeks. "I can't!"

Elizabeth frowned. How could anyone do something

that hurt so much when they didn't have to?

"I don't think I can drive home," Marabel said with a catch in her voice.

"I'll drive your car," said Elizabeth quickly. "We'll put you in Jill's and I'll follow you home."

"No!" Marabel shook her head. "Put me in my car." She looked up at Jill. "Honey, I love you, but I can't take your negative reaction right now."

Jill flushed and tears filled her eyes. Elizabeth blinked back tears of her own at the look on Jill's face. Jill really did love Marabel and it did hurt her to see her grandmother in pain.

With a groan Marabel sank down in the passenger seat of her car. "I didn't mean to upset you, Jill," she said and Jill turned abruptly away and walked toward her car.

Elizabeth called after her and she turned. Elizabeth tossed the ring of keys and Jill caught them, then almost ran to her car. Elizabeth sighed and slipped into Marabel's car and reached for the keys Marabel held out to her in a trembling hand.

"Maybe it's not worth it," whispered Marabel, dabbing away tears.

"It must be, or you wouldn't be doing it."

Marabel smiled weakly and Elizabeth turned to follow Jill.

At the house Jill waited stiffly near the back door to help her grandmother into the house. Elizabeth bit her bottom lip to keep from snapping at Jill as they walked with Marabel to the back door, through the kitchen, and to the living room where Marabel asked them to help her to the couch. She sat down with a sigh and leaned back.

"I really will be all right. I shouldn't have run so long, but I wanted to push myself a little more. I must run five miles!"

"Five!" cried Elizabeth and Jill together.

Jill dropped down beside her grandmother and Elizabeth sat on the plaid chair, leaning forward in anticipation.

"Why would you want to run five miles, Grandmother?"

Marabel clasped and unclasped her hands, then finally looked from Jill to Elizabeth. "I'm going to run in a race next week."

"A race?" asked Elizabeth, her eyes wide.

Jill gulped and shook her head.

"You don't have to tell me, Jill. I already know you'll object. But I am going to run the five-mile race and that's final!"

"Five miles?" whispered Jill. "Five miles!"

"Are you sure you can do it?" asked Elizabeth.

Marabel leaned forward. "I am going to do it! I settled that in my mind last year when I watched the race. I said then I'd be in the race next year. Well, I've been running almost a year now, and I'm going to be in the race."

Jill groaned and Elizabeth leaned back with a deep sigh. This was not at all what she'd expected to hear. She knew Jill was ready to burst, and she couldn't blame her. Running a five-mile race was different from running just for the fun of it.

Marabel tugged at the collar of her gray sweats. "I want to tell you how I feel so that you'll understand." She patted Jill's leg and Jill stiffened. "Your old grandmother hasn't gone off the deep end, honey. I just want to prove to myself that I can do what I've set out to do." She was quiet and Elizabeth heard a noisy car drive past; then the only sounds were their breathing and the tick of the marble mantel clock.

Jill reached for Marabel's hand and held it between both of hers. "I'm sorry for the way I've been acting, Grandmother. You have every right to do what you want. Even running. But I would like to hear why you're doing it."

Elizabeth pushed herself up. "I'll leave you alone. I think it's just between the two of you."

"Wait, Elizabeth," said Marabel. "You're here and you're involved. Please stay to listen. I do want you to and I'm sure Jill doesn't care."

"I don't." Jill smiled at Elizabeth and it was the first genuine smile that day.

Elizabeth sat down and leaned back and crossed her long legs. She picked a piece of grass off her jeans and held it.

Marabel pushed her fingers through her graying hair. "I must prove to myself that I can run this race. If I win, I win, but running it and finishing it are more important to me." She sighed deeply and her coloring was back to normal. She rubbed the calf of her left leg. "Leg, you can't give out on me now."

Elizabeth touched the crocheted doily on the arm of her chair and Jill moved restlessly.

With her head tipped and her blue eyes thoughtful, Marabel said, "I want to prove to myself that I can accomplish something that has been a desire of mine for many years. When Granddad was alive, he laughed when I said I wanted to run. I said I wanted to run in the Boston Marathon and he laughed harder. So I crawled into my shell and lived day by day the way Granddad expected me to live." She turned to Jill. "And you seem to think that I belong in my rocker all day long. Others feel the same. But I don't! I am as old as I feel, and I feel like running in the five-mile race, and I am going to do it! If I want to run in the Boston Marathon, I'll do that too!"

She crossed her trim ankles and folded her hands in her lap. "I started to run last year just after the race; then I hurt my ankle and I was forced to stop for a long time."

"Oh, Grandmother!" Jill rested her forehead against Marabel's arm. "What if you hurt yourself again? What if you break your leg, or something just as terrible?"

"I won't! I refuse to consider it! I am determined to run no matter what." She twisted around and cupped Jill's cheek with a small hand. "When you sit down to write your book, you don't know if you're doing it all for nothing. You don't know if it will sell or if it will be rejected, yet you keep on writing because you must." Marabel turned to Elizabeth. "And you keep on practicing your piano because you plan to be a concert pianist. You don't let anything get in your way. That's how I feel about running. I want to run and I will run! I want to show myself and others that I can accomplish something that's important to me."

"But why keep it a secret?" asked Elizabeth with a thoughtful frown puckering her wide forehead.

Marabel sighed. "I didn't want to give anyone the chance to talk me out of it. Jill, you almost did, but then I made myself continue."

"Do you think Pete would object?" asked Elizabeth softly.

Marabel shrugged. "He probably would. I won't take the chance. In many ways he's like Granddad. Pete will be at the race and then he'll find out. That's soon enough."

Marabel bit her bottom lip as she looked from Elizabeth to Jill. "I would like you girls to do something for me. I thought I could do this alone, but I can't."

"What, Grandmother?" asked Jill suspiciously.

"Help me run. I haven't run where the race will be held yet. I need to. I need to get used to running on a different surface from the track."

"What can we do?" asked Elizabeth, leaning forward in anticipation.

"We can't run," said Jill, shaking her head.

"You could drive the car or ride bikes beside me to keep me company. But mostly to encourage me." She plucked at the zipper on her jacket. "I sometimes feel like giving up. I want you girls to push me on. Will you do it? Can you?"

"Yes!" cried Elizabeth, her eyes sparkling.

"I don't know," whispered Jill.

Marabel reached for Jill's hand. "Please, honey. I do need your help. The race is next week. You and Elizabeth came here to help in the Country Cafe so that I'd be free to run. You didn't know it, but that's why I asked you to come. Now I'm asking—begging for more help."

Jill sat quietly, just looking at Marabel.

"We'll help her together, Jill," said Elizabeth softly. "Together."

Jill looked at Elizabeth, then finally smiled. "I'd like that."

"Can I count on you?" asked Marabel, her face bright with excitement.

"You can, Grandmother."

Elizabeth laughed happily and Marabel hugged Jill close. Elizabeth wanted to hug Jill also, but she sat still to give them time for each other. Maybe things would be better all the way around now.

She thought of Seth and the smile faded. How would she have time for Seth now that she'd promised to help Marabel?

SEVEN
Seth and Jill

She'd left a note propped up on the kitchen table that said, "I walked down to the lake. Be back soon. Elizabeth."

Would Jill guess that she was going to meet Seth, or was she too preoccupied with Marabel's running?

Elizabeth lifted her face to the warm morning sun as she waited to cross the street. A pickup with a boat in the back drove past; then she crossed and walked on the grass to the bank. She stopped near the large poplar and looked down at the sparkling blue lake. Seth wasn't there and she scanned the beach and spotted someone. Maybe it was Seth. Her heart leaped and she wrapped her arms around her reed-thin body.

She ran down the embankment, waving her arms to stop her pell-mell flight. Oh, but she hated to tell him that she couldn't stay!

He stopped and looked at her in surprise and she knew he was wondering why she was dressed in jeans and a tee shirt instead of a swimsuit.

"What's up? he asked, his hands lightly on his lean hips.

"I can't swim right now. I'm sorry."

He frowned. "Are you mad at me because of yesterday?"

She shook her head and her curls bounced. "I have to help Marabel. I promised that I would. I'll be free this afternoon."

"I have to work."

Her shoulders slumped. "I wanted to call you last night and then I realized that I didn't even know your last name. And I don't have your phone number."

He stuck his hands in his knit jacket pockets and laughed. "I didn't realize. It feels as if we've always known each other, so I didn't give it a thought."

"I've told you about me and the farm I live on and that I'm going to be a concert pianist, but you didn't tell me anything about yourself." She wanted to know everything about him. She wanted to know if he loved her as much as she loved him.

He tipped his dark head and his white teeth flashed as he smiled. "I am Seth Musanto and I'm nineteen. Marc and Karen are my parents and I have two younger sisters, Carrie and Betsy. We live over near the high school and we all love sports of any kind. In the fall I'm going to Tulsa to ORU to study medicine." He laughed again. "Did I leave anything out?"

"How old were you when you cut your first tooth?"

"Nine months."

"Then I guess that's all I need to know." It was hard to keep it light when she wanted to step into his arms and hear him say that he loved her.

He took her hands and held them and her heart

beat so loud that she was sure he could hear it. "All that information doesn't tell a thing about a person, Elizabeth. I think you know me and I know you and it has nothing to do with who our parents are or where we live or how old we are."

"You're right, Seth. I know that you are kind and helpful and you saved my life."

"I think you're wonderful for helping Mrs. Noteboom. She's a fine lady. All that running she does really keeps her in shape."

Elizabeth gasped. "How do you know she runs?"

"I've seen her several times. A couple of times I almost joined her, then decided she wanted to be alone."

"Do you think it's terrible that a woman her age is running?"

Seth laughed and shook his head. "You're asking the wrong person. My whole family runs. Do you, Elizabeth?"

She shook her head and wrinkled her nose. "I hope you don't think less of me. I do play tennis once in a while and I ride. But running is not for me."

"Does Jill run?"

Elizabeth stiffened. "No. Why do you ask?"

"She could keep Mrs. Noteboom company. Running alone can get lonely, and when you aren't in shape, it causes a lot of aches and pains."

Elizabeth watched a bird fly toward the poplar. A motorboat roared into life and sped across the lake, making waves that washed up onto the sand. Finally she looked up to meet Seth's eyes. "Jill and I are going to help Marabel by riding bikes along beside her so she can run on the race track."

"Race track?"

Elizabeth bit her bottom lip. "Marabel wanted to keep it a secret, but since you know about her running, I guess I can tell you. Promise not to tell anyone."

"I promise."

"She's going to run in the five-mile race next week."

"Great! So are we! Does she know the route?"

"Yes. She told us last night and we're going with her this morning. That's why I can't swim with you. I really have to get back or they'll think I deserted them." She didn't want to leave. She wanted Seth to hold her hands forever, but she slowly tugged free and he let her go.

"How about tonight?"

"We're going with her again tonight." He sighed. "And I work all day. We can't let this happen to us, Elizabeth. We have something precious and we don't want to lose it."

The words wrapped around her heart and warmed her. "What can we do?"

"We could meet here about six each morning."

Six? Could she crawl out of bed that early? For Seth she could do anything. She nodded. "I'll be here."

He smiled, then said, "See you at six in the morning."

She turned and walked away and forced herself to keep walking when she wanted to turn back to him and stay and forget about her promise to Marabel. Six o'clock in the morning really would come, even though it seemed a long way away.

She ran the last few yards and reached the back door just as it opened and Jill stepped out.

"I was just coming to get you, Elizabeth. We're

ready." Jill glanced suspiciously over Elizabeth's shoulder. "Where were you anyway?"

"Didn't you read my note?"

Just then the door opened and Marabel stepped out, once again dressed in the gray sweatsuit. "Good. You're back, Elizabeth. We're ready if you are."

"I'm ready." She couldn't meet the accusing look in Jill's eyes as she walked with Jill to get the bikes from the garage.

Marabel closed the garage door after them and Elizabeth stood beside the ten-speed, waiting for Marabel to tell them what to do.

"Jill, you have an odometer on that bike. You tell me when I've run two and a half miles so that when I run back, it'll make it five miles. If I can't make it, Elizabeth, you come back for the car."

"You'll make it," said Elizabeth with a firm nod of her head.

"Today I'll run from here along the lake road. To-morrow I'll run the race track." She smiled with confidence and Elizabeth was proud of her.

"Grandmother," said Jill softly and Marabel turned to her. "I do want you to succeed. I know it's impor-tant to you. I just wish I could run along beside you, but I know I'd conk out at a quarter mile. I do my best work at my typewriter." She laughed and Marabel hugged her, then started running down the drive and onto the lake road.

Elizabeth smiled at Jill and she smiled back. They were working together and Elizabeth knew their jealousy over Seth would be set aside for a while. She was glad. It was terrible to be upset with Jill and have her upset in return.

At two miles Jill handed Marabel a Thermos cup of orange juice and told her how far and how fast she'd run.

"Keep up the good work," cried Elizabeth, who was standing just ahead of them at the side of the road with her bike.

At two and a half miles Jill told Marabel that it was time to turn and run back. Marabel wiped perspiration off her forehead and Elizabeth handed her a cup of water.

"I know I'm going to make it," said Marabel cheerfully. "With you girls helping me, I can do it!"

"Sure you can," said Elizabeth.

Jill pedaled faster, her back stiff. A small dog ran along beside her, barking furiously. She ignored him and he finally fell back and ran off across the field away from the lake. A pheasant whirred and flew up and away.

At four miles Marabel slowed considerably and Jill handed her another cup of juice.

"I don't know if I can make it, girls," Marabel gasped.

"Sure you can," said Elizabeth from behind Marabel.

"I'll walk and you can ride this bike," said Jill, stepping off the ten-speed.

"No!" shouted Elizabeth, pedaling fast until she was beside Jill. "She can make it, Jill! Leave her alone!"

"She's tired and she hurts," cried Jill, her face flushed with anger.

Elizabeth watched as Marabel continued to run along the side of the road. "Watch her, Jill. She can make it."

Jill's eyes narrowed. "I wish you would mind your

own business," she hissed. "What harm would it do for her to ride the rest of the way?"

"I won't fight with you, Jill. You make me so angry because you won't understand, but I won't fight and upset your grandmother."

"Oh, listen to the sweet, pure girl. You think you're so good, don't you? I wish you'd never come with me to Grandmother's!"

A car drove toward them and they were forced to move to the side of the road. Elizabeth glared at Jill and pedaled off toward Marabel.

Elizabeth's heart raced in anger and she wanted to stop the bike and yell at Jill, but she pedaled until she was beside Marabel. Her face was flushed and wet and she was almost at a walk.

"It's not far, Marabel. You can do it! Even if you have to walk the last few feet, you can make it!"

Marabel nodded and ran again, her shoes thudding on the pavement. Her breathing was ragged and Elizabeth wanted to tell her to stop and ride back, but she bit her tongue and wouldn't let the words out. How could she help Marabel? Suddenly Elizabeth smiled. She knew what she could do.

"God is my strength," sang Elizabeth in her unsteady soprano. "God is my strength and my help. A help in time of trouble."

Marabel flashed her a smile and Elizabeth continued to sing all the way to the back door of Marabel's house.

Marabel sagged against the door and Elizabeth leaped off her bike and before she could reach Marabel, Jill was helping her inside. Jill wouldn't look at Elizabeth and she wanted to tell her just what she thought of her. Elizabeth kept the sharp words back but the anger burned inside.

She thought about the Scripture verse in James that said blessing and cursing came from the same mouth, and that it shouldn't be that way. She flushed and her stomach knotted. She had every right to be angry at Jill.

Elizabeth walked to her bedroom and slammed the door shut. Was she being like Jesus? He wouldn't get angry with Jill and yell at her one minute, then sing a Scripture song to Marabel the next.

Elizabeth moaned and covered her face as she sank down on the edge of her bed.

"Forgive me, Jesus. I'm sorry. I don't mean to get upset with Jill, but I just can't help myself. Please, help me."

Several minutes later, dressed in blue slacks and a white knit shirt with blue flowers around the scoop neck, Elizabeth walked out of her bedroom to go with Jill to work at the Country Cafe.

Jill wasn't in the living room or kitchen. Elizabeth tapped on her door, then pushed it open. The bedroom was empty. Splashes came from the bathroom where Marabel was soaking in a tub of warm water. Elizabeth sighed. Jill hadn't waited. She'd gone ahead to the Country Cafe. Maybe Jill wouldn't want to have anything to do with her. Maybe she should just go home and forget about helping Marabel.

But what about Seth?

Elizabeth sighed as she walked outdoors. No matter what, she'd stay until it was time to go home. She'd help Marabel and Jill. She'd see Seth and be with him as much as she could in the little time they had.

As she opened the front door of the Country Cafe the bell tinkled and Jill looked up from where she stood at the cash register, taking money from a customer. She didn't smile or acknowledge Elizabeth.

Elizabeth lifted her pointed chin and walked toward the gift shop to help two people near the fabric frames. The warm aroma of bacon frying and bread toasting drifted from the kitchen where Elizabeth knew Mr. Bailer was at work.

The bell tinkled and Elizabeth watched John Bogart walk in. Once again he was dressed in shorts and a tee shirt. His dark hair was combed neatly. He lifted his hand to Elizabeth, then sat down at a small table and watched Jill. He looked as if he had something on his mind.

"Good morning. May I help you?" asked Jill without a smile, her pad in one hand, a pencil in the other.

"I want to talk," John said in a low voice that barely reached Elizabeth's ears.

"I'm busy. If you want some breakfast, I can help you. Otherwise, I can't." Jill stood stiffly, her pad poised.

"Cup of hot chocolate and wheat toast with peach jelly," snapped John.

Jill scribbled, her face red, then turned and walked toward the kitchen.

Elizabeth slowly walked to John and stood behind a chair across from him. "Hi. What's going on?"

"That friend of yours hates me. What have I done to her?"

"You should know. Your name is Bogart and right now she's upset with anyone by that name."

"Is she always so abrupt and stern?" He looked back

75

where Jill stood at the opening between the dining area and kitchen.

Elizabeth frowned, then shook her head. "I've never seen her act this way before. We're supposed to be best friends, but I can't get along with her either."

Jill cleared her throat from just behind Elizabeth. Elizabeth looked around quickly and flushed painfully. "You have a customer, Elizabeth."

Elizabeth nodded and walked stiffly to wait on the woman who stood at the gift shop counter, holding a stuffed mouse with a piece of swiss cheese between its front paws.

In a few minutes the place was empty except for John, Elizabeth, Jill, and the cook in the kitchen. Elizabeth picked up a feather duster and walked slowly around dusting the gift shop items. She could hear John and Jill as they sat together at the table. John had finished his hot chocolate and toast.

"I told Grandpa I'd try harder to get to know you and Marabel, and I mean to do just that," John said crisply. "You aren't helping at all. Your friend said that you're a nice girl."

Jill looked quickly toward Elizabeth and she dusted harder.

"I know that I want Grandmother to have a good life. Why does she need to include your grandpa? She has a family. We love her. She could come live with us, but she won't because of this cafe and gift shop."

"Let's get off that and talk about you. Tell me about yourself. I really am interested." John smiled and Jill sat straighter and clasped her hands in her lap.

The door opened and a bell tinkled. Elizabeth hurried forward to wait on the woman customer before Jill jumped up to do it. Jill and John needed to sit and talk. Just maybe they'd become friends.

Elizabeth smiled to herself. Maybe Jill would become interested in John and forget about Seth. Maybe.

EIGHT
End of a friendship

Elizabeth drove Marabel's car slowly down Norway Avenue straining her eyes for 1262. Was Seth home right now? Would he look out his window and see her drive past? She fidgeted nervously with her purse on the seat beside her. What would he think of her if he knew that she'd deliberately set out to find his house so that she could see where he lived?

Finally she found 1262 Norway Avenue and she laughed with excitement. Seth lived in that white house with the charcoal gray shutters.

She turned around in a neighboring drive, then slowly crept back to pass the house again. Three girls were standing on the sidewalk, talking, and they glanced toward Elizabeth's car; a flush crept up her neck and over her face. What if they knew what she was doing? Wouldn't they giggle over that?

As she drove past again she noticed a red Chevy parked in the drive. She hadn't spotted it before. She gasped and her eyes widened in surprise. The red

Chevy belonged to Jill Noteboom! Why was Jill at Seth's house?

Elizabeth gripped the steering wheel tighter and clenched her teeth. With a jerk she pulled to the curb about a block from Seth's house. She leaned her head weakly against her trembling hands on the steering wheel. Had Seth been leading her on the past few days? Was he really in love with Jill?

Elizabeth groaned. Were Seth and Jill talking and laughing about that strange girl, Elizabeth Johnson, who thought she was in love with him? Had he told Jill about saving her life? Had he told Jill how she'd clung to him?

Elizabeth's face burned. Had Jill been laughing behind her back over Seth Musanto?

Or maybe Jill was making a play for Seth and he didn't want her to!

Elizabeth's head shot up and she gripped the steering wheel so hard that her knuckles turned white. She should rush into Seth's house and grab Jill and pull her out of there!

No wonder Jill had asked Marabel for time off from work!

Elizabeth glanced at her watch. She had only twenty more minutes before she had to get back to help with the supper crowd. Jill had to be back the same time.

A fly buzzed through the open window and landed on Elizabeth's bare knee. She brushed it off, then rubbed her damp palms on her shorts. The hot afternoon sun shone brightly in the side car window. A girl that Elizabeth had met in church Sunday walked past the car and Elizabeth slumped low. Music drifted from a small yellow house.

Finally Jill walked out of the house to her car. She was alone. Elizabeth strained her eyes to catch the expression on Jill's face, but she was too far away.

Jill backed out and drove away and finally Elizabeth pulled away from the curb and drove around the block and home. She felt numb and had to force herself to concentrate on her driving.

She could not put off the serious talk with Jill that she'd mentioned a few days ago. This had to be settled. Her pulse quickened and her palms were wet with perspiration.

Jill's car was empty as Elizabeth parked beside it. She flung open the door and strode rapidly toward Marabel's house.

She slammed the back door behind her and yelled, "Jill! Where are you, Jill?"

Jill rushed in, her face pale, her dark eyes wide. "What is it? Grandmother? What?"

Elizabeth doubled her fists at her sides and her chest rose and fell in agitation. How innocent Jill sounded!

"I saw your car, Jill!"

Jill frowned. "So?"

"At Seth's! I saw you there and I want to know why you were there. How dare you spend time with Seth? He's my boyfriend, not yours!"

Jill stepped forward, her eyes blazing, her fists doubled at her sides. "I like Seth and if I want to see him, it's my business, not yours! You don't own him, Elizabeth Gail Johnson! I don't know how you can say he's your boyfriend. He likes me best, and I know it! You're nothing to him! You haven't even gone out with him."

"But I have! We've walked together and swum together."

"Has he kissed you?"

"No, but . . ."

"But what?"

Elizabeth walked to the kitchen table and gripped the back of a chair. "Has he kissed *you?*"

Jill lifted her head high. "He will. We just haven't had a chance to be alone."

"Ah-ha!" Elizabeth shook her finger at Jill. "You haven't been alone with him because he doesn't want it that way. He made a way to be alone with me. He said he didn't want to lose what we have."

Tears filled Jill's eyes and one at a time spilled down her pale cheeks. "I don't believe you."

Elizabeth felt a touch of sympathy for Jill but she pushed it away. "I am telling the truth."

The hum of the refrigerator broke the silence that followed. Finally Jill turned away, her shoulders bent. "You have everything, don't you, Elizabeth? Grandmother loves you more than me because you don't object to her running. And you like Pete, too, and that pleases Grandmother. Seth probably does like you better than me. I've been terrible ever since I learned about Grandmother's running, as well as having Pete in her life. But I can't seem to help myself."

Tears filled Elizabeth's eyes and she took a step toward Jill, then stopped as Jill spun around.

"I wish you had stayed home, Elizabeth! I could have talked Grandmother out of running! I could have had Seth to myself! I could have broken up Grandmother and Pete!"

82

Elizabeth stared open-mouthed at Jill, then ran past her to the bedroom and slammed the door hard. She flung herself across the bed, face down and sobbed into her pillow. Jill hated her! Jill didn't want to be friends any longer.

Finally the tears stopped and Elizabeth sadly pushed herself up. She had to go to work no matter how she felt, no matter how much Jill hated her.

Several minutes later Elizabeth walked across to the cafe. She was dressed in a yellow flowered sundress and it swirled around her knees at each step. Her feet felt cool in white sandals. She hesitated at the door, knowing Jill was already inside.

The aroma of fried chicken met her as she walked inside. Today's specialty was fried chicken, potato salad with a relish plate and a choice of fresh peas or green beans.

Most of the tables were full and Jill already looked rushed as she took orders at a table near the gift shop. Elizabeth glanced at Jill, then looked quickly away.

"Hi, Elizabeth," said Marabel with a wide smile. "We can certainly use you. Pete's coming later so we can have supper together."

"That's nice."

"Is something wrong, Elizabeth? Your eyes are red. Have you been crying? Are you homesick? Or over-worked?"

"I'm OK, Marabel."

Marabel hugged her and Elizabeth could smell the faint scent of lilac perfume that Marabel wore. "You're a dear girl and I love you, Elizabeth. Thank you for the way you've helped me. I'll never forget it.

If there's anything that I can do for you, let me know."

Tears blurred Elizabeth's vision and she quickly blinked them away as she forced a smile. "Thank you. I think I'd better get to work right now. We have some hungry-looking customers."

Marabel looked at her strangely, then turned away and Elizabeth found her pad and pencil and walked to the table that was assigned to her.

Much later Pete walked in and Marabel showed him to a corner table, then hurried to the cash register to take the money from a couple who were waiting to pay and leave.

Elizabeth saw Jill frown at Pete but he was watching Marabel and didn't see the frown. Elizabeth stepped close to Jill and whispered, "Leave Pete and Marabel alone, can't you? They need each other. You're being such a big baby over the whole thing."

Jill clamped her mouth closed tightly and marched away, her head high, her back stiff.

Just then a customer needed Elizabeth's help in the gift shop and she hurried to assist. Marabel's table was in full view and Elizabeth was close enough to hear what Pete and Marabel were saying to each other.

Elizabeth didn't want to listen, but she couldn't help herself. Even after she waited on the customer, she stayed in the gift shop.

"I know Jill doesn't want us together," Pete said earnestly.

"I'm sorry, Pete. It isn't anything personal. She just doesn't want me to consider marrying again."

"And are you?"

Marabel flushed and looked down at her hands, then at Pete. "Yes."

He smiled. "So am I. You might as well know that John feels the same as Jill. He wants me to go home with him and stay there."

"Oh, Pete!"

"I know. It would be hard to be apart from you."

"I care about you, Pete. We share so many things."

He moved his fork. "Except maybe one thing."

"What's that?"

"Your running."

She gasped and Elizabeth stood still, her eyes wide, trying to hide the fact that she was listening.

"Who told you, Pete?" asked Marabel with a catch in her voice.

"Someone at church. I wanted to say something sooner but I didn't have the courage."

Elizabeth held her breath as she saw the stricken look on Marabel's pale face.

"And what did you want to say, Pete?"

"I want you to be very careful and not push yourself too hard. You're too important to me." He reached across the table and caught her hand in his. "I guess I'm just old-fashioned enough to think it's undignified for a lady to run, especially a lady our age."

Marabel pulled her hand free. "Old-fashioned is right! Women have been running in races for years and years. Where have you been?"

Elizabeth knew Marabel was angry. Could Pete tell how angry? He'd have to be very careful or he wouldn't have a dinner companion very long, nor a friend.

"It's not dignified, Marabel."

"Who cares? Haven't you ever done something that isn't dignified?"

Pete laughed and reached for Marabel's hand but she pulled away. "I'm sorry if I hurt you. I love you and I want you to be happy. If running makes you happy, then run, but please be careful. I don't want you to hurt yourself."

Marabel lifted her chin defiantly. "I'm running in the race tomorrow, Pete."

He gasped and his ears turned red. "That's five miles!"

"I can do it."

"Please don't, Mari."

She leaned forward. "I am going to!"

Elizabeth bit her bottom lip and tried to walk away, but she wanted to hear the outcome.

Pete didn't speak for several seconds. "I can see that this is very important to you. I can't understand why, but I love you and I want you to do what you want to do."

Marabel gasped and tears filled her eyes. "You won't try to talk me out of the race?"

Pete shook his head. "No. It wouldn't be right."

"Thank you. It is very important to me and I will do it!"

Elizabeth turned away, smiling happily. Somebody was happy and she was glad. Too bad she and Jill couldn't work out their disagreements. But Jill would never take back her words.

With a shrug Elizabeth walked to the counter. She hadn't done anything wrong to Jill. *She* wasn't the one that needed to apologize. *She* wasn't the one that should make the first move.

Her stomach fluttered strangely and a great sadness swept over her. She and Jill had been best friends for a long time. It was hard to lose her. Maybe the friendship wasn't to be. Maybe she had outgrown Jill.

Elizabeth looked toward the table where Jill was waiting on two women. The sadness on Jill's face brought tears to Elizabeth's eyes. She blinked rapidly. She wouldn't feel sorry for Jill! She had brought it on herself.

The bell tinkled and Elizabeth looked toward the door. Her heart leaped as Seth walked in. He said hello to Jill, then looked around. His dark eyes met Elizabeth's and a thrill ran over her. She smiled and he smiled.

He stopped in front of her. He was dressed in faded jeans and a blue tee shirt. "Hello."

"Hello," she whispered.

His eyes darkened with an emotion that sent her pulse leaping. "I had to come see you, Elizabeth, since we can't meet as usual in the morning because of the race."

"I'm glad you came. Shall we sit down?"

He nodded and she led him to one of the empty tables. Jill shot an angry look at her but she turned away and sat beside Seth.

"Are you and your family ready for the race tomorrow?" she asked.

"Yes. How about Mrs. Noteboom?"

"She's ready. She had a little trouble this morning, but I think she'll be just fine tomorrow."

Seth laced his fingers through hers. "Jill came to see me today to ask if we could get together after the race."

Elizabeth gasped and sat very still. "What did you say?"

"That I already have plans. This will be the last chance for you to meet my family before you go home. Mom is planning a big dinner for all of us."

"I hope they like me."

Seth grinned. "Who wouldn't?"

She could name a few. "Will I see you in the morning before the race? I want to wish you the best. I want you to win."

"Thanks. I won last year and I have a good chance this year. I'll try to find you before the race, but it'll be very crowded. Most of the townspeople plus the tourists will be there. But I'll look for you."

They talked for a few more minutes, then Elizabeth stood up. "I do have to get back to work. I'll see you in the morning. Thanks for coming now."

He smiled a heart-stopping smile, then turned and walked out.

Finally Elizabeth turned to go back to work. The look on Jill's face stopped her short. Elizabeth flipped her hair back and looked down her nose at Jill. If Jill wanted an all-out battle, then that's just what she was going to get!

NINE
Friendship renewed

Elizabeth walked restlessly across the living room. She knew Marabel was still in the bathtub, soaking after tonight's run. Jill was in the bedroom with her door locked. She might as well have hung a "No Trespassing" sign on it. Elizabeth frowned. Of course the sign would only be meant for her and not Marabel. For that matter any human being in the world would be more welcome than she.

She sat at the piano and tried to play but her fingers felt stiff and not at all like her own. She wiggled them and tried to play again. She sounded the way she had when she'd first started taking lessons from Vera.

"What is wrong with me?"

The words hung in the air and slowly she turned and stood up. She knew what was wrong. She missed Jill. She missed the talks and the laughter and the sharing. Jill was like a dear sister, not just a girl who lived down the road from the Johnson farm.

Elizabeth stood at the front window and looked out

into the night. Lights cast a yellow glow over the street and lawn. She remembered the first time that she'd seen Jill and it was as clear as if it were yesterday. She'd been twelve and Jill already thirteen, a very tall, big thirteen. She'd been lying in a ditch "experiencing" what it would be like to be knocked out and lying in a ditch. Elizabeth had never met anyone who had talked as much or asked as many questions. She'd said she needed to know everything because she was writing a book. She'd kept it locked in a box and hidden at the back of her closet.

Elizabeth smiled. That seemed so long ago! Was she ready to give up the good friendship she'd had with Jill the past five years?

She looked toward the doorway to the hall and wondered what Jill was thinking and feeling right now. Maybe the broken friendship didn't bother her.

Marabel walked in, tying the belt of her lime green robe. It touched her lime green slippers and swirled around her slim ankles as she walked to Elizabeth. "You look as if you've lost your best friend, Elizabeth."

Elizabeth flushed. "I think I have."

Marabel looked over her shoulder, then back at Elizabeth. "I thought something was going on. I hoped it would pass, but it seems to be worse than ever. I believe it's time to sit down and have a long talk."

Butterflies fluttered in Elizabeth's stomach. "Marabel, I don't think Jill wants to talk."

"We'll see about that!" Marabel strode to the hall and Elizabeth heard her knock on the bedroom door and call for Jill.

Elizabeth turned back to look out the window. An

icy band tightened around her heart and she wanted to run out the front door away from the confrontation. Jill hated her and maybe she always would.

At the sound of steps behind her Elizabeth stiffened. How could she turn and face Jill?

"Sit down, girls," said Marabel firmly.

Elizabeth finally turned. She saw Jill's red eyes and nose and knew she'd been crying a long time.

"Sit down, girls," said Marabel again in a voice that demanded obedience. "We aren't going to spend another minute with this black cloud over our heads."

Elizabeth sat on the plaid chair and watched Jill fold her robe around herself and sit on the couch with Marabel.

"I don't know what caused the tension between you two, but it shouldn't be." Marabel looked from Jill to Elizabeth. "We're Christians and we're learning each day how to be like Jesus. Something is happening here that we need to take care of. James 3:16 says, 'For where envying and strife is, there is confusion and every evil work.'

"You girls are in strife and that leaves an opening for Satan to work. We don't want that."

Elizabeth sank deeper into the chair and clutched a beige throw pillow. She had forgotten about that Scripture. She certainly didn't want to allow Satan to do anything destructive in her life or in Jill's.

Jill looked down at her hands folded in her lap. Color stained her cheeks. The marble mantel clock chimed ten.

Marabel crossed her legs, then held her robe closed over her knees. "Girls, 1 John 1:9 says that when we sin, we are to confess our sins and Jesus will forgive us and make us clean. You're both such fine Christian girls that I know you'll want to do that. You don't want sin to block your fellowship with your heavenly Father."

Elizabeth struggled to keep back tears. Later, in her room she'd cry all she wanted, but not now, not in front of Marabel and Jill.

"I want to pray with you girls, and then I'll leave you alone to work this out. Just remember that friendship is important. A true friend isn't always easy to find. A true friend will stick with you no matter what the circumstances. I know that you girls are true friends."

Elizabeth peeked at Jill who wouldn't look up, then closed her eyes and pressed the pillow tighter to her stomach. Inside, tears fell fast, washing away the anger and bitterness and even the jealousy.

"Heavenly Father, thank you for your Son Jesus," prayed Marabel. "He became sin for us so that we wouldn't have to carry the punishment of sin. Forgive us for any wrongdoing and cleanse us from all unrighteousness. Thank you that you said that you'd forgive and forget our sins. We want to be more like Jesus day by day. We want to be a shining example of Jesus every day. Thank you, Father, that your love is shed abroad in our hearts by the Holy Ghost so that we can love with your love. We refuse to give Satan a place in our lives. God, you are our Father and we love you. In Jesus' name. Amen."

Elizabeth quickly brushed tears from her lashes and smiled at Marabel as she stood up.

"Girls, talk it out and settle it," said Marabel softly. "Call me when it's done and we'll have cocoa in the kitchen before we go to bed."

Jill shifted so that her back was against the pillow at the corner of the couch. "Thank you, Grandmother," she whispered hoarsely.

Marabel leaned forward and kissed Jill's damp cheek, then turned around and kissed Elizabeth. She smelled clean and fresh.

Elizabeth crossed her ankles as she watched Marabel walk away. Finally she turned to Jill, who was studying her intently. Elizabeth cleared her throat. "I am sorry, Jill. I didn't mean to hurt you."

Jill twisted her fingers together and sniffed hard. "Me either. I love you, Elizabeth. I never hated you. Well, maybe when I was so mad."

"Your grandmother really doesn't love me more, Jill."

"I know. I understand now. I still don't like to see her run because of the pain it causes her, but I didn't have any right to try to force her to stop. And I shouldn't have been angry with you over it. Forgive me?"

"Yes. And forgive me for yelling at you." Elizabeth tried to bring up Seth, but his name stuck in her throat.

Jill pushed herself up and walked to the front window and looked out, then turned around. "What really happened to us, Libby?"

Her old nickname brought memories rushing back. She and Jill had had so many good years. Would she let Seth come between them now?

"What do you think, Jill?"

Jill moistened her full lips with the tip of her tongue. She plucked at a button at her neck. "I think I love Seth Musanto."

Elizabeth gasped and leaped up. "Oh, Jill, no!"

She nodded, tears glistening in her brown eyes. "I saw him at the lake a few days after we first came here. I walked right up to him and talked to him and he talked to me as if I were really important to him."

"That's his way."

Jill flushed. "Are you saying that he doesn't love me?"

Elizabeth walked behind the chair and gripped the back of it. "He doesn't, Jill. But not because you aren't wonderful and all that."

"Does he love you?" Jill asked stiffly.

Elizabeth nodded. "I think so."

"So, he's going to come between us no matter what."

Elizabeth trembled. "We won't let him come between us."

"Do you love him?"

"Yes."

Jill pressed her hands to her head. "This is terrible! We're in love with the same guy."

"Do you really love him, Jill?" Elizabeth's stomach knotted.

"I think I do, Libby."

"Do you want me to step aside and give you a chance with him?"

Jill wrapped her arms across her slender body. "I couldn't do that even if I wanted to. But what are we going to do?"

Elizabeth slowly walked to Jill and slipped her arms around her. Jill's arms closed around Elizabeth and they stood together, sobbing quietly.

What could they do?

Finally they sat on the couch and turned to face

each other. Jill rubbed her hair back from her slender face and Elizabeth wiped away her tears.

"Do you remember when I was in love with Adam Feuder?" asked Jill with a soft laugh. "I got so upset when I thought you were in love with him, too."

"I remember. I wasn't even interested in Adam."

"But you are interested in Seth."

Elizabeth swallowed hard. "Yes."

Jill twisted a curl around her finger. "What are we going to do?"

"Next week we'll be home and none of this will have any significance. We can't think about only now, Jill." Elizabeth rubbed the arm of the couch as her stomach knotted painfully. "I'll give up Seth if that's what you want." Oh, how could she?

"Oh, Elizabeth!"

"You are more important to me than anyone else right now, Jill. I do love Seth, but if you and I can't be friends because of Seth, then I will give him up."

Jill blinked hard and pressed her lips together tightly. "I'll give him up, also."

A band tightened around Elizabeth's heart and squeezed until she wanted to cry out. How could she tell Seth that she'd never see him nor speak to him again? How could she tell him that she couldn't go with him to visit his family and have dinner with them?

"Elizabeth, remember how fat and ugly I used to be?"

"I didn't think you were ugly."

"Well, I was. Sometimes I still think that I'm fat and ugly and that no boy will look at me. I think that's why I wanted Seth to like me. He's so handsome! He's smart. He's everything that I'd like in a boy."

"He wants to be a doctor."

"I didn't know that."

"I was going to have dinner with his family tomorrow after the race. I haven't met them before."

"I have. His sisters are beautiful and nice, too." Jill sighed. "I wanted so bad for him to like me!"

"He saved my life."

Jill's eyes snapped wide and her mouth dropped open. "What?"

Elizabeth nodded as she locked her icy fingers together in her lap. She told Jill about the boat accident, her struggle to stay above water, her fight with Seth before she realized that he was trying to save her. But she didn't tell that he'd held her until she'd stopped crying, that she'd comforted him or that they'd hated parting. "I thought for sure that that was the end of me," she said unsteadily. "But I asked the Lord for help and he sent Seth."

"Oh, Elizabeth! Oh, what would I have done if you'd drowned?" Jill shuddered, then reached for Elizabeth's hand and squeezed it tightly. "Grandmother told me that a true friend is hard to find. Elizabeth, you are my true friend."

Elizabeth smiled through her tears. "I'm glad, Jill."

Marabel poked her head into the room, her brows lifted. "All settled, girls?"

"Yes," said Jill and Elizabeth nodded.

"Then, let's go have a cup of hot cocoa." Marabel beckoned to the girls and they followed her to the kitchen. She poured milk into a pan while Elizabeth took out the can of cocoa mix and Jill the cups. They

talked quietly and Elizabeth could feel the peace
around them that had been missing for days.

When the cocoa was ready, the three sat down at
the kitchen table. Elizabeth rubbed her finger around
the rim of her cup. She liked the look of the melting
marshmallow in the hot cocoa.

Marabel gave a sigh. "Girls, I helped you; now it's
your turn to help me."

"What can we do, Grandmother?"

Marabel sipped her cocoa slowly, then set the cup
down. "My stomach is full of butterflies. I think I'm
going to pull out of the race."

"No!" cried Elizabeth.

"You can't, Grandmother," said Jill, shaking her
head. "You've wanted to do this for a long time. Don't
back out just because you're nervous."

Elizabeth smiled at Jill. "Good advice."

"Grandmother, you said winning didn't matter, but
running did. You have to run. I think you should even
try to win. Wouldn't you like that?"

Marabel grinned, then laughed aloud. "I certainly
would! Why should I just run to run? I can run to
win! I'll pick up my color and my number in the morning and I'll run that race to the best of my ability!"

"And we'll be there cheering you on," said Elizabeth.
She looked at Jill. "Together!"

"Together," said Jill softly.

Marabel's blue eyes filled with tears. "I'm certainly
glad to hear that."

Later Elizabeth pulled the flowered sheet over her
and her head sank into her pillow. My, but she was
tired. The alarm was set for seven instead of six for
her usual meeting with Seth.

"Oh, Seth," she whispered. She turned her face into her pillow and wept. How could she walk up to him in the morning and tell him that she couldn't see him again?

But she had to do it because of Jill.

"Heavenly Father, give me the strength to say good-bye to Seth. I don't want to, but for Jill, I will. But only with your help, Father."

The tears fell faster and wet her pillow.

TEN
Victory

The fragrance of popcorn and coffee filled the air to blend with the odor of several hundred people pushing and shoving to find a front row seat for the race. Elizabeth watched them and shook her head in amazement.

"Can you believe this, Jill?"

"It's a good thing we got here at eight. It's too bad we didn't bring chairs like these others did."

Elizabeth nodded absently as she strained to catch sight of a black-haired, black-eyed boy with a beautiful smile. Her throat felt tight and hot tears threatened to fall. She wanted to see Seth, yet she dreaded to.

"Here comes Grandmother!" Jill grabbed Elizabeth's arm and jumped up and down excitedly, her curls bouncing.

Elizabeth's hazel eyes sparkled as she watched Marabel push through the crowd toward them. Marabel was dressed in red and white shorts and a

tank top with ankle socks. A yellow sign with the large number 36 covered her chest. A yellow ribbon with the black number 36 was pinned to the corner of the sign. Her blue eyes were bright with excitement and her cheeks glowed with happiness.

"I'm really here!" she cried as she hugged the girls together. "I'm finally going to run in a race!"

Elizabeth kissed her cheek, then stepped back to give Jill time alone with her. Jill was dressed in faded cutoffs and a light blue tee shirt.

Just then a hand gripped Elizabeth's arm and her heart dropped to her feet. She prickled with heat even though she was dressed in shorts and a tee shirt. Oh, she couldn't see Seth now!

She turned her head hesitantly, then smiled in relief to see Pete with John beside him.

"We came to cheer Marabel on," said Pete with a grin.

"She'll be glad to see you." Elizabeth smiled at John, then noticed the blue tag with the number 43 on his chest. "John! I didn't know you were going to run today." She clutched Jill's arm and tugged her around. "Look! John's running too."

Jill's eyes widened. "Are you sure you should, John?"

He laughed. "It won't be my first race."

"But why didn't you say something about it?" asked Jill.

He shrugged and grinned. Then he sobered and looked right into Jill's eyes. "Will you cheer me on?"

Elizabeth smiled a secret, knowing smile as she backed away a couple of steps.

Jill flushed. "Yes, I will, John," she said softly.

He smiled into her eyes, then turned to speak to

Marabel before he walked away to get into the crowd of runners.

Jill turned to face Elizabeth. "I think he likes me! Did you see the way he looked at me? Did you hear him ask if I'd cheer him on?"

Elizabeth chuckled. "Why are you so surprised? Like grandfather, like grandson."

Jill wrinkled her nose. "Oh, Libby!"

Just then Pete turned to Jill. He had an arm around Marabel and she had her head against him. She looked ready to burst with happiness. "Jill, we want you to share our good news." He smiled at Elizabeth. "And you, too."

"Maybe I can already guess," said Jill softly.

"Maybe so," said Pete. "But we'll tell you anyway. Marabel and I are both going to run in this race next year."

"What?" Jill blinked in surprise.

Elizabeth looked at Marabel and she winked.

"Your grandmother has convinced me that running a race is exciting and rewarding. We'll be running as Pete and Marabel Bogart."

Jill gasped, her hand at her mouth; then she squealed and hugged Marabel and kissed Pete's cheek and Elizabeth did the same.

"I have to go now," said Marabel. She took a deep breath. "Oh, dear! I'm really here and I'm really going to run. Can I do it? My stomach is full of butterflies."

"You can do it," said Pete and Elizabeth at the same time.

"Sure you can, Grandmother," said Jill, giving Marabel a quick hug. "Now go join the other runners."

Tears blurred Elizabeth's eyes as Marabel hurried

away through the crowd. She wiped her eyes just as someone caught her arm and spun her around. She looked up to see Seth smiling at her, a large blue tag on his chest with the black number 25.

"I had to see you, Elizabeth," he whispered.

She couldn't speak around the lump in her throat as she looked into his dark eyes.

He pulled her close and kissed her and her lips tingled and her heart leaped. Before she could collect her wits, he turned and walked through the crowd away from her. She touched her lips and tried to catch sight of him again.

He had kissed her and she had to tell him that she was finished with him. She looked helplessly at Jill, who was talking earnestly with Pete. Why, oh, why had she told Jill that she'd give Seth up?

She had, and she'd stay by her word for Jill, her best friend.

Elizabeth blinked back tears and moved out of the way for a mother pushing a stroller with twins. The shoving and shouting and smells were almost overwhelming to Elizabeth. She wanted to stand close to Jill and talk with her, but Jill was too involved with Pete.

Suddenly it was time for the race and Elizabeth's stomach tied into hard knots as she heard the loud crack of the gun. She cheered and it blended together with all the other cheers. She was cheering for Seth and Marabel and John, even for the other runners. And if someone in the race had no one to cheer for him, she cheered for him. She laughed and waved her arms high and cheered again. Maybe she should take up running and run in a race at home next year, if there was one.

The excitement in the air was like an electric charge

and Elizabeth had to hold herself back from running with the runners in this race. She laughed and her hazel eyes sparkled and her cheeks flushed a bright red.

Jill touched her arm and she turned with a laugh.

"Isn't this great, Jill? Wouldn't you like to be in the race?"

Jill laughed. "Not on your life! I couldn't make it. I'm glad there are aid stations along the way so Grandmother can get a drink."

"I hope she beats her own time."

Jill nodded. "Yesterday she did sixty-one minutes. Pete told me that John runs five miles in twenty-five minutes."

"The weather is perfect for the race, not too hot and not too cold. I know Marabel will run well."

The crowd thinned out and Elizabeth and Jill walked slowly to the tape across the finish line. The runners had to run down Campground Road, across Page Street, then up Lapeer Street to end back at the beginning. Marabel had run it three times without the streets being blocked off. Today she would make better time. Elizabeth looked at the tape and pictured Marabel breaking through it, her hands up, her chest forward. She would make it. She had to.

Elizabeth looked up the street to see crowds gathered on both sides for as far as she could see. How much longer before they could spot a runner? Her nerves tingled as she thought of Seth crossing the finish line. Would he come to her after he handed in his tag and learned his time?

"Elizabeth?"

She turned to Jill, her brows raised questioningly.

"I saw Seth kiss you."

Her stomach tightened. "Did you?"

"Yes." Jill licked her lips. "Did you . . . tell him?"

"I couldn't. Not then."

"Are you going to?"

She wanted to cry. "Yes, Jill."

Jill nodded without smiling and Elizabeth looked back up Lapeer Street. She blinked and strained her eyes. Was someone coming?

A shout went up and she knew it was someone. But who? She saw a man with binoculars and she wanted to rip them from his hands and use them herself.

"I wonder if it's John," said Jill in a strained voice.

"Or Seth," whispered Elizabeth under her breath so that even Jill couldn't hear.

The crowd cheered louder but Elizabeth's throat closed and she couldn't make a sound. She locked her fingers together and waited, her chest rising and falling as if she'd just run ten miles.

Instead of one runner she saw that it was three and they were almost side by side. It was Seth and John and a girl. It was going to be close!

The cheering increased until it was a roar inside Elizabeth's head. Jill jumped up and down beside her, shouting with the others, but still she couldn't push a sound through her mouth.

Just then the runners seemed to hit the tape at the same time and Elizabeth knew that only the time-keepers would be able to tell the winner.

Perspiration dotted her forehead as she watched Seth hand his ribbon to a timekeeper; then he turned and looked around until he spotted her. He smiled and her heart stood still.

"Go to him, Elizabeth," said Jill in a low, tense voice.

"I was wrong. You don't have to give Seth up to keep my friendship. Go to him and tell him he's wonderful!"

Elizabeth looked blankly at Jill.

"Go!" Jill shook Elizabeth's arm, then pushed her and finally Elizabeth got the message. She grabbed Jill and hugged her, then ran toward Seth as he ran toward her.

He caught her and held her and she held him and cried a little and laughed a little.

"I'd better catch my breath," he said as he walked to an open grassy spot and sank down.

She sat with him and held his hand and waited until he was breathing normally. She could smell his tangy perspiration and hear his thudding heart or maybe it was her heart. She laughed and he grinned, his eyes flashing with excitement.

"I think you won, Seth."

"I think so, too."

The crowd roared again and Elizabeth tried to look through the many legs to see the street. "Maybe Marabel is coming in now."

Seth shook his head. "She'll be at least fifteen more minutes." He pushed himself up and she jumped up with him. "Let's watch the race, shall we, Elizabeth?"

She nodded as he held her hand and walked with her back to stand with Jill and John.

"Good race, John," said Seth, holding out his hand to shake hands with John.

"You too, Seth."

"We're first and second in our class and Sally Everett was third," said Seth. "We'll have to wait to hear who was first."

"Where is Grandmother?" asked Jill, shielding her eyes to see farther.

"It'll be a while yet," said John. "She'll make it. Don't worry about that. I saw Grandpa at the four-mile aid station. He's going to cheer her on when she passes it."

"I'm glad," said Jill. "Did you know that they're going to get married in September?"

"Grandpa told me."

"Are you upset?"

"I'd still like to have him come stay with us, but since he won't, then I'm glad that he'll have Mrs. Noteboom. I like her."

"Me, too." Jill laughed. "And I like Pete, too. I'm sorry that it took so long before I did."

Elizabeth listened to them and couldn't believe they were the same two people that had been so angry about Marabel and Pete. Marabel had said that where strife was, other evil things were at work. The enemy had certainly been busy keeping everyone at odds. But no longer!

"You look very pleased, Elizabeth," said Seth close to her ear.

"I am! I'll tell you later when we're alone."

"Look! Here come my sisters!" cried Seth. He cupped his hands around his mouth. "Come on, Carrie! Come on, Betsy!"

"Carrie! Betsy!" shouted Elizabeth, jumping up and down.

Several minutes later the girls stood with Seth and he introduced them to Elizabeth. They both had black hair and eyes just like Seth.

"Seth said that you'd play the piano for us today," said Carrie.

Elizabeth nodded.

"We're looking forward to having you with us for the day," said Betsy.

Elizabeth smiled and caught Jill's eye and smiled at her for being a real friend and giving this to her when she'd thought she'd lost it.

"There's Mom and Dad!" shouted Carrie, bouncing up and down.

Elizabeth shouted with the others as she watched the man and woman running toward the finish line. Both of them had black hair and eyes. He was tall and she was short. They looked at each other as they ran, then looked straight ahead until they were over the line with shouts of congratulation ringing around them.

Seth excused himself and he ran with his sisters to his parents. Elizabeth rubbed her damp palms down her shorts. Soon she'd be meeting Seth's parents. She looked around for Jill and saw her with John, pushing their way up Lapeer Street. Had they seen Marabel?

Elizabeth glanced at her watch. Marabel had been running forty-five minutes. Was she all right?

Silently Elizabeth prayed for strength for Marabel as she ran.

"Why the frown?" asked Seth as he slipped his arm around her.

She grinned sheepishly. "I'm a little concerned about Marabel. I want her to finish almost as much as she wants to."

"She will. Right now I want you to meet my parents." Seth smiled proudly. "Mom and Dad, this is Elizabeth Johnson. Elizabeth, Marc and Karen Musanto."

Elizabeth shook hands with them and tried to say all the right words. They talked to her a while, then walked away with Seth's sisters.

"Do you think they liked me, Seth?"

He squeezed her waist. "Of course."

A man nearby lit a cigar and the smoke drifted across Elizabeth and she coughed. Jill and John rushed up and Elizabeth grabbed Jill's hand.

"Did you see your grandmother?"

"Yes! She's coming and her time is the best yet!"

More and more runners crossed the finish line but so far none with yellow tags. But then almost in front of Elizabeth's eyes was a man with a yellow tag. He was going to get the best time for the yellow group. Her heart sank and she leaned her head against Seth.

"I know how you feel," said Seth.

"What do you mean?"

"You saw the man with the yellow tag and that means Marabel won't be first. But at least she's running and she will come in. There are a lot of people who don't even finish the race. There are a lot of people who don't have the courage to enter in the first place."

"Elizabeth!" cried Jill. "Here she comes!"

Elizabeth reached for Jill's hand and held it and they stood together, side by side, and waited for Marabel.

"She looks so tired," whispered Jill. "She's limping!" cried Elizabeth. "One of her socks is down."

As Marabel drew closer, Elizabeth could see her scratched and bloody knee and leg. Elizabeth pressed her hand to her mouth and almost stopped breathing.

Marabel stumbled and the crowd gasped. She caught herself and ran slower.

"Come on, Grandmother!" shouted Jill. "You can make it!"

Elizabeth saw the tears running down Marabel's cheeks and she wanted to rush out on the street and help her finish the race.

"Faster, Grandmother!" shouted Jill and Elizabeth stared at her in surprise.

"She can't go faster, Jill," snapped Elizabeth. "She's hurting."

"She wants to win, Elizabeth. She wants to run, but she wants to win. She'll make second place if she runs faster. Do you know how proud she'll be if she makes second place?"

Elizabeth bit her bottom lip and nodded slightly.

"Faster, Grandmother!" shouted Jill again, then again.

Marabel lifted her head and increased her speed just as Elizabeth spotted a man with a yellow ribbon just behind Marabel. If he got ahead of Marabel that would push her to third. Third wasn't bad, but Marabel would want second since she couldn't have first.

"You can do it, Marabel!" shouted Elizabeth. She jumped up and bumped into Seth and he smiled at her and she smiled back.

"Marabel!" they shouted together.

"Grandmother!" shouted Jill and John joined in.

All the hours and hours of practice have paid off, thought Elizabeth as she watched Marabel's legs pump up and down and her arms swing back and forth.

"Faster, Grandmother!" screamed Jill. "Faster! Faster! You're almost there!"

Suddenly Marabel burst across the line, with the other yellow runner behind her.

Marabel had come in second! She'd run the race and she'd won!

Elizabeth hugged Jill and they jumped and danced and shouted; then Jill pulled away and ran to Marabel. Elizabeth looked at Seth with tears running down her cheeks. He pulled her close and held her and she let the tears of happiness fall.

ABOUT THE AUTHOR

Hilda Stahl was born and raised in the Nebraska Sandhills. When she was a young teen she realized she needed a personal relationship with God, so she accepted Christ into her life. She attended a Bible college where she met her husband, Norman. They raised their seven children in Michigan where she lived until her death in 1993.

When Hilda was a young mother with three children, she saw an ad in a magazine for a correspondence course in writing. She took the test, passed it, and soon fell in love with being a writer. She wrote whenever she had free time, and she eventually began to sell what she wrote.

Hilda published books with Tyndale House Publishers (the Elizabeth Gail series, the Tina series, the Teddy Joe series, and the Tyler Twins series), Accent Books (the Wren House mystery series), Bethel Publishing (the Amber Ainslie detective series, and *Gently Touch Sheela Jenkins*, a book for adults on child abuse), and Crossway Books (the Super JAM series for boys and *Sadie Rose*
and the Daring Escape, for which she won the 1989 Angel Award). Hilda also had hundreds of short stories published and wrote a radio script for the Children's Bible Hour.

Some of Hilda's books have been translated into foreign languages, including Dutch, Chinese, and Hebrew. And when her first Elizabeth Gail book, *The Mystery at the Johnson Farm*, was made into a movie in 1989, it was a real dream come true for Hilda. She wanted her books and their message of God's love and power to reach and help people all over the world. Hilda's writing centered on the truth that, no matter what we may experience or face in life, Christ is always the answer.

Hilda was featured speaker on writing at schools and organizations, and she was an instructor for the Institute of Children's Literature. She continued throughout her life to write, teach, and speak—but mostly to write, because that is what she felt God had called her to do